Desperate Trek:

One Family's Journey from Honduras to Texas

By Cynthia Roman, Ed.D

ISBN 978-1-62806-256-4 (paperback)
ISBN 978-1-62806-257-1 (ebook)
ISBN 978-1-62806-258-8 (ebook)

Library of Congress Control Number 2019914040

Published by Salt Water Media
29 Broad Street, Suite 104
Berlin, MD 21811
www.saltwatermedia.com

Edited by Mary Lib Morgan

Table of Contents

ACKNOWLEDGEMENTS

I would like to thank the following people:

Jim Wieboldt – my husband, whose support and encouragement kept me going on a daily basis. He patiently read and commented on every chapter, making sure that a reader would understand my thinking. Jim's ability to ask good questions and insist that I fact-check everything kept me on the straight and narrow writing path.

Mary Lib Morgan – my new friend and editor, who not only made me sound better but helped me translate my outrage over the immigration crisis at the southern border into a story that anyone would want to read. Thanks for having the willingness to make that 5-hour drive the first time, Mary Lib!

Jeanne Schlesinger of JeanneS Unique Lens – Thanks to my talented illustrator who captured the ongoing journey of Jorge, Maria, and Sofia by providing a visual representation of their challenges traveling by foot.

Salt Water Media – especially Andrew Heller, Stephanie Fowler, and Patty Gregorio. What a treat to work with such friendly pros!

Virginia Bianco-Mathis – my long-time friend, business partner, and mentor. She challenged me to "go deeper" and let my readers inside the hearts and souls of my characters.

Jacqueline Poliquin – my friend, who noticed issues in the story that many others had missed. Thanks for your eagle eye!

The First Saturday Writer's Club of Berlin, Maryland – They gave me early encouragement and feedback when I read them the very first chapter. Their ongoing interest and support are gratefully received.

Al and Maritza Wieboldt – my brother-in-law and his wife. Al, who is a retired publishing executive and Maritza, who is a native of Columbia, offered perspectives I couldn't have otherwise accessed.

You, my cherished reader – May you be encouraged by this book to ask hard questions when something doesn't sound accurate; to be vigilant to events that violate your values; and to show compassion to those who suffer extraordinary hardships.

Most of all, I want to acknowledge the migrants from Central America, who have more to teach us about courage, hope, and determination than we can imagine. Thank you and welcome to America!

INTRODUCTION

I have fond memories of regular trips to the public library when I was growing up. Like many young girls of my generation, I loved Nancy Drew mysteries and Walter Farley books about horses. I checked out 10 – 12 books at a time, especially in the summer, and devoured them as quickly as possible. When I attended the University of Virginia for my undergraduate degree, I majored in English and read even more. I learned how to analyze literature and developed better writing skills. However, my graduate education took me in the direction of management and organizational development, changing my reading habits for the next 40 years.

Never in my wildest dreams did I imagine that I'd be writing a novel for the first time at age 65. As a retired university professor and management consultant, I'm no stranger to writing. I co-authored several books and wrote dozens of articles designed to help leaders become more effective. However, academic articles and professional reports are a far cry from fiction.

I had missed the opportunity to read for pleasure throughout my career. Because of my work, I read a lot of management and business literature, but I never seemed to have enough time to read fiction. So I decided that one of my top goals during retirement was to explore all the books I had wanted to read earlier in my life. I joined two book clubs and read both the best-sellers and the classics. Once again, reading became my refuge and the fuel for my imagination. At the same time, I became interested in the growing field of mindfulness. Meditation and journaling became important parts of my daily routine and I taught mindfulness at a local library. My mindfulness practice brought a level of self-acceptance and ability to trust my insights that I'd never before experienced.

I have always been a news junkie, probably due to my dad's influence. He was a newspaper editor, so current events were a daily source of family discussion. My political leanings to the left and my father's conservatism made for some interesting conversations in my younger days. When the current U.S. president began spewing lies about the growing number of migrants from Central America and advocating a wall as a solution to the immigration crisis, I felt a rush of sympathy for these desperate people and believed my father would have, as well. I read everything I could find on the plight of the migrants. I became incensed at the lack of concern for the impact of the government's new immigration policies on the growing number of families trying to cross the border into the U.S. My heart and soul told me that I needed to do something. Writing a "nonfiction novel" seemed to be the right fit for me. I decided to go for it.

A "nonfiction" novel combines elements of fact with fiction. While the Hernandez family featured in Desperate Trek is purely fictional, their day to day struggles are based in fact. Everything in their journey from Honduras to Texas has actually occurred to hundreds of migrants. You will find references at the book's conclusion supporting what Maria, Jorge, and Sofia experience. The story does not take place at a fixed point in time; rather, it reflects what my research showed as general ongoing and worsening issues that have faced migrants over the past several years. As I began writing this story, my trepidation at writing fiction was quickly dispelled. The Hernandez family's desperate trek to a better life in the U.S. practically wrote itself. I had no guiding outline, no predetermined outcome. I just had a very human family faced with extraordinary hardships. I was careful and thorough with my research; the story is a universal saga of human need, resilience, and hope. We all could be Maria, Jorge, Sofia, and even Miguel. History is replete with the story of immigration. We are all immigrants, trying to create better lives for our families.

The major frustration I faced in writing this story was the changing landscape of and response to the current immigration crisis. I often felt as if every article I read contradicted the previous article. But, in fact, that is the reality of this current crisis. The knee-jerk government reaction to rapidly changing immigration events not only thwarts any kind of long-term planning; it increases confusion and possible error in the way the agencies respond. The complexity of the immigration crisis and the grinding bureaucratic government processes are mind-boggling. And it just keeps getting worse.

I don't have an answer and can't yet suggest solutions. My hope is that a focus on one family's experience will provide a different perspective from the fear mongering that certain media outlets promulgate and perpetuate daily. Even more important, I hope this story will provoke readers who have not yet become alarmed to start talking about all the issues in the current immigration crisis rather than continuing to bury their heads in the sand. Frankly, while I'm a lifelong dog lover, I'm tired of seeing cute pictures of puppies on social media when thousands of migrants are fleeing life-threatening violence in their home countries. We can do better. We must do better.

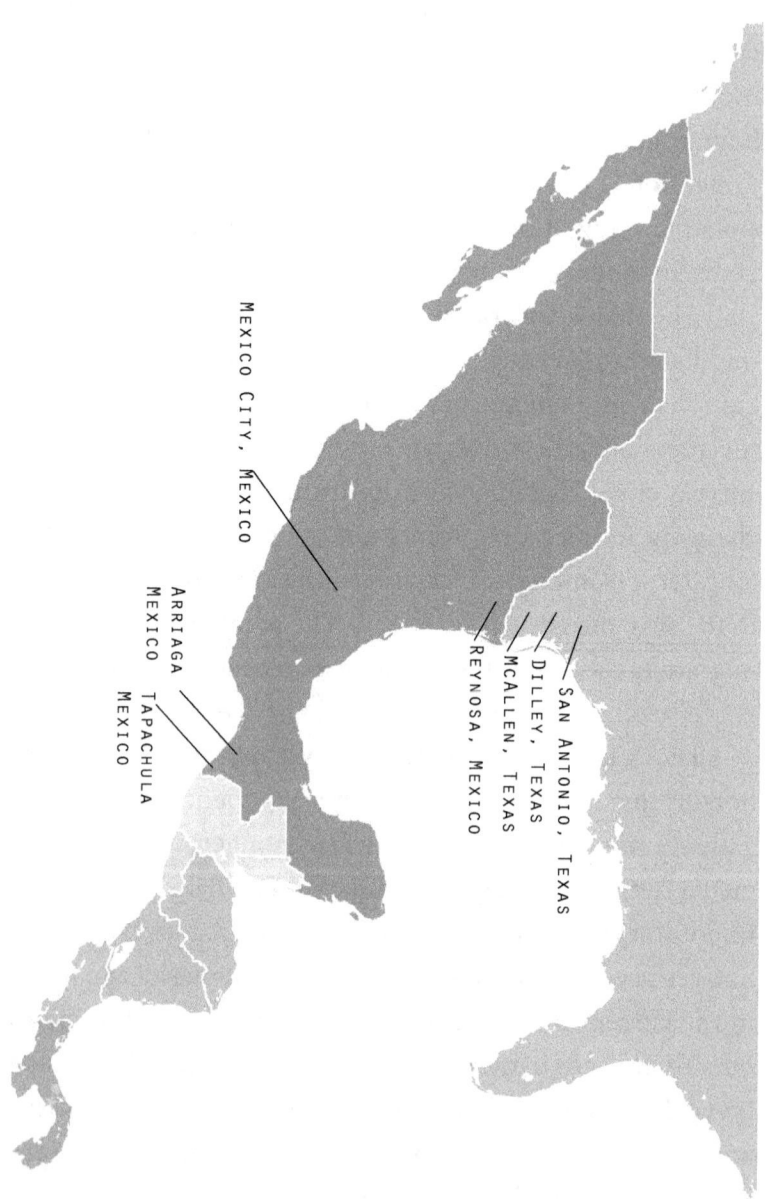

MEXICO CITY, MEXICO

ARRIAGA
MEXICO

TAPACHULA
MEXICO

SAN ANTONIO, TEXAS

DILLEY, TEXAS

MCALLEN, TEXAS

REYNOSA, MEXICO

PROLOGUE

THE TERROR BEGINS

Jorge called the police from his cell phone, but he knew Miguel was dead. He also knew the police would make little effort to investigate.

They didn't always live with terror in their lives. Maria Lopez Garcia remembers how her mother would often take her and her brother to the park to play on the slides and watch the neighborhood boys play soccer. When she was a child, they walked through the neighborhood without fear and often stopped to talk with other families who lived near them. They had all that they needed in the community and at home - even a TV. Maria loved watching cartoons with her brother. They watched two shows every day after they did their chores.

Maria's father was a truck driver and, although he was gone a lot, he was always home on the weekends. Maria's fondest memories of her father were after Sunday dinners when he sang songs to her while she sat on his lap. While her family didn't have much money, they were never hungry. Maria's mother took pride in her cooking, especially in her *pastelitos de carne*,[1] which she made for the family every Sunday.

Life started to change in Maria's neighborhood when drug traffic to the U.S. laid the foundation for a dramatic transformation in Honduran society. Rival gangs fought over control of drug territories, sometimes block by block. Their violence drove out many businesses offering legitimate employment, including the trucking company where Maria's father worked. Government corruption and lack of resources led to weak enforcement of laws. Gang members and drug smugglers operated with impunity for crimes, both serious and petty. Members of the community who did not pay their *war tax*[2] protection to the gangs were threatened and often killed for their stand against extortion.

After Maria's father was laid off from his job, the family struggled to survive. His efforts to find work were futile as the shops closed and many neighbors began leaving their town. When she was fifteen, Maria dropped out of school to help her mother with occasional cleaning jobs. It hurt them both to be cleaning for wealthy drug smugglers, but they had to take this work or go hungry.

Maria's only brother, Miguel, turned fifteen and immediately joined the local gang, following in the footsteps of most of his friends. Miguel's small salary for the war taxes he collected was paid by his gang boss. This illegitimate income together with the meager mother-daughter income from cleaning gave the family a means for survival.

Maria met Jorge Hernandez Ramirez when they attended

---

1 Small, crispy meat pies traditionally served in Honduras

2 Widely varying amounts of money extorted from individuals, small businesses, the public transportation sector, and churches by gangs in exchange for life, safety, and/or continued functioning of business

the same school. Jorge lived a few miles away from Maria on a small farm; he was far less affected by gang violence than Maria's family and all the townspeople. Jorge's family lived in poverty like so many of the other people in rural Honduras. They owned a small plot of land and subsisted largely on what they grew and made fresh at home - corn and tortillas, plantains, and beans. Jorge's father earned daily wages of about $4.00 on a nearby farm while his mother worked at home. Jorge attended school in town; his parents hoped he would complete secondary school and enroll in college. After only a few years in elementary school, his sisters dropped out to help their mother since she suffered ongoing respiratory ailments and was often unable to complete routine household chores.

The Catholic Church and its various agencies played a large part in Jorge's family life. A home nursing arm of the church provided support when Jorge's mother was ill. A rural agricultural development charity helped improve their water and sanitation systems. The church also provided funds for Jorge to attend secondary school since free education ended with elementary school.

By the time Jorge was eighteen and had known Maria for several years, his dream of attending college was long gone. There was no money to pay for school; besides, he and Maria wanted to get married. Jorge moved in with Maria and her family after he finished secondary school. He found work as a day laborer around town. When he had saved enough money for the marriage license, he and Maria got married at the town hall. This was hardly the wedding of Maria's dreams; rather, it almost seemed an afterthought.

Nine months later, Maria had a baby girl they named

Sofia. Maria doted on her baby and took care of her ailing parents while Jorge worked at various day labor jobs. Sometimes he assisted on construction projects; other times he worked in an auto repair shop. Over several months, his skills had improved notably, and the few employers left in town appreciated his expertise and reliability. Jorge was determined to resist the temptation of joining a gang even though the money was alluring. He managed his honestly earned money carefully, always trying to save a small portion of his meager wages. He and Maria dreamed of eventually owning their own home.

Miguel protected Jorge from gang intimidation, but Maria worried about their safety every day. Miguel's earnings from gang work and Jorge's day labor wages combined were barely enough to feed and shelter the entire family. This burden was felt deeply by both Miguel and Jorge; they pledged that they'd find a safer means of support than illegal activity, but Miguel acknowledged the reality that the gang now essentially owned him.

As Maria and her mother were preparing dinner late one summer afternoon, shots rang out. While the gunfire itself was not unusual, these shots were nearby. Maria's heart jumped into her throat as she rushed to the front door. Jorge was running toward her, yelling her name. When he reached her, Maria knew what had happened before he breathlessly shared the awful news. Less than a block from their house, a crowd was gathering around a motionless body in the street. When Maria reached her brother lying face down, she saw that he had been shot multiple times. The pool of blood spread quickly as Maria and her parents bent down to cradle Miguel, Maria's mother wailing and calling out his name. Jorge called the police from his cell phone, but he knew Miguel was dead. He also knew the police would make little effort to investigate.

Miguel's murder touched off a new gang war in the neighborhood. One or more gang members stood guard on almost every street corner, daring rival gangs to trespass into their territory and demanding a fee from anyone walking down the street. Refusing to comply meant threats of rape or murder. Jorge began to vary his daily routes so he could avoid gang members, but they knew he lived at Maria's home. They began to harass the entire family.

Over the next few years, there were the expected ups and downs. Some days were better than others. The Hernandez family learned to survive in uneasy coexistence with the drug gangs now entrenched in their town. When Maria's father passed away, her mother stayed home to take care of Sofia while Maria continued to clean homes. Time seemed to fly by; Sofia grew into an energetic five-year old.

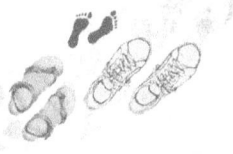

CHAPTER 1

LEAVING HOME

With nothing other than the clothes on his back and pure determination, Jorge put Sofia on his shoulders and waded into the water.

Sofia held her doll close as the throngs of people pushed and shoved their way across the long, narrow bridge that connected Guatemala to Mexico. Maria had tied a leather cord to her waist, and she pulled Sofia close as they struggled to stay together in all the chaos. Sofia looked up at her mother and asked, "Mama, is North America at the end of this bridge?" Maria brushed the hair out of Sofia's face and said, "No, we still have a long way to go to get there."

She looked up to see Jorge - about twenty feet ahead of them - stumble and fall, spilling his backpack onto the bridge. Frantically, Maria grabbed Sofia's hand and tried to reach Jorge before he was trampled by hundreds of others in the caravan.

Jorge caught Maria's eye and smiled. He was fine but his backpack's contents didn't fare as well. When he had passed a fruit stand earlier, he bought a few bananas and tomatoes for their lunch. Now the fruit lay totally smashed under the feet of his fellow migrants on the bridge. As he pulled himself up, Jorge tried to put on a brave face for the benefit of his wife and daughter, but inside his frustration was mounting. *How much longer could they endure this?* Nine days ago, they left their hometown in Honduras and had faced tremendous challenges in their journey ever since. Heat and exhaustion were a problem for everyone, especially for Maria. She was five months pregnant, and Jorge could see that she was in pain. Her ankles were badly swollen, and she had several large, angry blisters on her feet.

The Hernandez family's dire circumstances began a year earlier when Honduran gangs ratcheted up their neighborhood violence once again. Jorge continued to work as a laborer whenever and wherever he could find work, but it was a struggle to feed his family, especially after Miguel's murder. When the gangs wanted Jorge to get involved in drug smuggling, he was tempted. The local gang initially promised him good pay and ongoing jobs. Maria, however, argued that Jorge should not trust these assurances. She knew from stories she had heard from family members in other parts of town that gang promises quickly became threats. Maria begged Jorge to lead them north, away from the violence and fear. Finally, when she told Jorge she was pregnant again, he knew that he had to move his family to a safer area. What he didn't tell Maria was that a gang member told Jorge that if he didn't start working for them, Maria would be raped, and maybe killed. Jorge knew they had to leave now.

Maria's mother refused to leave her home, but Jorge, Maria, and Sofia joined a caravan of several hundred migrants who began their trek north from Honduras. Marching through their home country, they found strength and solidarity with their fellow Hondurans, all hoping for a better life in the U.S.

Maria and Jorge anticipated that crossing the border into Guatemala would be easy. An "administrative border," the border between Guatemala and Honduras was usually open and unguarded. However, news of this huge caravan had spread to the Guatemalan authorities and much farther north into the U.S. Pressure from the U.S. government prompted Guatemala to send police to the Honduran border to stop the caravan. Maria and Jorge, who were near the front of the group, were dismayed that their journey north could be halted before it had barely begun. The standoff lasted several hours before authorities backed down, and the caravan continued its way north through Guatemala. The migrants cheered and waved flags from their home countries as they progressed across the border. Like everyone else, Maria and Jorge were inspired by this success to think even more optimistically about their chances of crossing the border into the U.S.

Already numbering in the hundreds, once inside Guatemala the caravan swelled with additional migrants from the impoverished western areas of the country. Decimated by a 40-year civil war that ended in 1996, the region's indigenous people suffered disproportionately from homelessness, poverty, lack of jobs, and gang-related violence. Faced with disappearing opportunities, many of these Guatemalans believed their only option was to leave. They traveled in small groups to the main roads leading north to Mexico. Many of the small groups joining the caravan were families with small children, hoping they would be safer by traveling with a larger group.

A week later, the group numbered in the thousands. Their walk across Guatemala was hard but their hopes for a better life in the U.S. kept them going. Maria made friends with other migrant mothers and they kept each other's spirits up, often singing and sharing family stories as they plodded along. Families sat around roadside campfires at night and shared their hopes for their children to get an education and lead better lives in the north. For the first few days, Sofia rarely spoke and held tightly to her mother's hand. As the days wore on, however, she began to join in the happy songs and laugh joyfully with her new friends.

As the caravan passed through Guatemalan villages, some residents shouted encouragement and even offered water and food. Jorge was grateful, but he knew that they would not be greeted so warmly at the Mexican border. As he listened to stories of migrants who were deported from Mexico back to Honduras, he began to worry. He knew that they couldn't go back to their home. Maria was exhausted, but he had to figure out a way to persist. If they could just get across the border into Mexico, Jorge thought they could get a ride across the country. If that didn't work, maybe he could get a job in Mexico. Anything was better than going back to Honduras.

Jorge, Maria, and Sofia paused briefly to take in their surroundings. At long last, they were making their way across the bridge between Guatemala and Mexico. Jorge felt adrenaline surging through his body as he heard the police whistles on the Mexican side of the border. Through the crowd he could see a phalanx of police advancing toward them. It appeared that the authorities were not going to allow the caravan to use the bridge that crossed into Mexico. For a brief moment, Jorge considered his options – advance to meet the police with their tear gas and armor, wait for direction from the police, or turn and run back to the Guatemalan border. He looked at Maria, then, lifting Sofia up and holding her tightly in his arms, shouted to his wife, "Follow me!"

Along with dozens of other migrants, the family retreated to the Guatemalan border. Jorge saw fellow sojourners climb down the bank and begin wading across the shallow river. With nothing other than the clothes on his back and pure determination, Jorge put Sofia on his shoulders and waded into the water. Knowing that this was their only chance, Maria followed, forgetting that her feet were on fire. The first of the group who stepped onto the far shore planted his tired feet firmly in place. All who followed then formed a line and began passing the children over to the Mexican side. Maria grabbed Sofia, placing her into the hands of a complete stranger and shouted above the din, "Don't be scared, Sofia. Wait for us on the shore. Be brave!"

By the time Jorge and Maria were able to reach Sofia on the other side of the river, their fellow migrants were already stripping down to their underwear and hanging their wet clothes on the trees that lined the shore. Maria hugged Sofia as her fears began to subside. Jorge looked around him and was surprised to see that no police were there to arrest them. They were in Mexico! He looked up at the bridge to see police officers looking down at them, like tourists watching animals at a zoo. But they didn't seem to be heading toward the shore. Were they really going to let the migrants stay in Mexico?

Jorge, Maria, and Sofia sat down on a log to catch their

breath and ponder their next move. They knew that the journey through Mexico would be filled with danger, but right now they needed to rest rather than worry. Drenched and without a change of clothing for her daughter, Maria wrapped Sofia in a small damp blanket from her backpack. After a while they joined the other families around a campfire that the men were tending. It was going to be a long night.

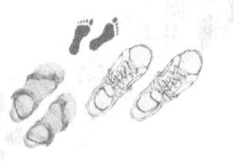

CHAPTER 2

MEXICO

All of Maria's alarm bells went off – she had been warned not to go with anyone who offered help.

As if the three bedraggled migrants weren't wet enough after trudging across the river, showers persisted through the night. It had been impossible to dry out or get much sleep by the struggling fire on the river's shore. Early the next morning, Jorge, Maria, and Sofia scaled the river bank and walked into the town of Tapachula, just inside the border of Mexico. They sat in the sun outside a small café and watched as police walked toward the border and shop owners opened their businesses. Maria and Jorge had a light breakfast of juice and tortillas as they assessed their surroundings. Sofia was sleeping peacefully in her mother's lap, and Maria was beginning to relax, but Jorge was vigilant as he surveyed the migrants and townspeople mingling in the streets.

Soon, a small group of migrants approached Jorge and asked if the family wanted to join them in traveling north across Mexico. Jorge didn't hesitate because he knew there was more safety in numbers than if he ventured alone with his wife and daughter. The men discussed their options and reached a consensus: the dangers that awaited them in Mexico would make their trek across Guatemala seem minor in comparison. Assaults, robberies, and abduction were common. Corrupt Mexican police were known for their attempts at extortion and their mistreatment of migrants. Despite the dangers, the group decided to stay together and try to catch the train to Arriaga.

Maria didn't try to talk Jorge out of this decision. After all, she was the one who initially wanted to join the caravan. But now, she was worried. Every bone in her body ached, and her feet were so swollen that she could hardly squeeze into her sandals. Sofia was coping better than Maria thought she would, but the throngs of fellow migrants often overwhelmed and frightened her. Maria was also worried that her child wasn't getting enough good food to eat. How could they make it across a country as large as Mexico? Before walking to the train station in Tapachula, Maria found a thrift shop and bought a pair of sneakers for Sofia. She also bought a looser pair of pants for herself. Her belly seemed to be getting bigger every day.

The next day, the family joined the others at the train station. Once more they strained against the crowd of migrants, all wanting to climb the freight trains going north. It was there they learned the devastating news. The Beast[3] wouldn't be running for at least the next five days and perhaps longer. When Maria heard this news, she couldn't hold back her tears. She slumped on the train platform and

---

3   A network of freight trains running north through Mexico to the U.S. border, providing illegal transport for as many as four hundred migrants per trip.

sobbed, Sofia in her arms. "What are we going to do?" she wailed to Jorge.

Jorge dropped their large duffel bag next to Maria and sat down on top of it. He didn't know how to answer his wife. He didn't know what they were going to do. It seemed as if Mexico's new, tougher immigration policies were going to prevent them from ever reaching their dream of a better life in the U.S. After comforting Maria, he told her to stay on the platform while he took some time to think and figure out their next steps. "Maria, this will work out; you'll see. I'm going to see what I can find out from others in the caravan."

For the next couple of hours Jorge wandered among the migrants, asking questions and listening for any information that might help them settle on a new strategy. While he was some distance away from Maria, a group of Mexican police and an immigration officer approached Maria demanding that she leave the platform immediately. Frantically, she scanned the crowd for Jorge to no avail. The immigration officers offered to take her and Sofia to a shelter. All of Maria's alarm bells went off – she had been warned not to go with anyone who offered help. At that instant, she saw Jorge and screamed his name. He ran over to Maria and turned to the officers.

"We are a family – this is my wife and daughter." He yelled over the noise on the platform. "We will stay together and I would like to find a job," Jorge added. "Can you help us?"

The immigration officer saw that Maria was pregnant and in distress. He mentally calculated how much room remained at the closest shelter and decided to bump this family to the top of his list. "Follow me," the officer said. "I will take you to a city shelter where you can rest and get food."

Maria whispered in Jorge's ear, "Can we trust him?"

Jorge replied, "Yes," though he really had no idea who he could trust anymore. He scooped up Sofia and grabbed the duffel bag with his right hand, while Maria donned her hat and struggled to get to her feet. She followed her husband and the officer as they left the shaded platform and began to walk the hot city streets to the shelter.

The immigration officer wanted to help these migrants. He knew they were desperate and had few, if any, options. While this caravan was overwhelming in size, he had dealt with migrants heading to the U.S. for years. Many of them had family already in the States, and all they wanted was to work and provide an education for their children. This caravan was different. It was gut-wrenching. He had never seen so many mothers and children running from violence in any previous caravan. He knew it was getting harder to survive the trek north. The Beast would soon be shut down permanently, and smugglers were ratcheting up their fees so that now few could afford them.

The shelter was little more than a cinder block box with bunk beds. Jorge, Maria, and Sofia were assigned two beds and shown the bathroom and where meals were brought in. While Jorge talked with the immigration officer about where he might find work for a few days, Maria and Sofia joined other mothers and children on the adjacent playground. For the first time all day, Sofia let go of her mother's hand and ran to the swing set.

Five days later the family returned to the train station, relieved to find The Beast ready for a trip to Arriaga. However, this was to be no ordinary train ride. Most migrants didn't have enough money for train fare, nor did many of them have the necessary immigration papers. Jorge and Maria were no exception. Along with hundreds of other migrants heading north to the U.S. border, the only way they could travel by train was to climb to the top of the freight cars. It was never a guarantee that the Mexican officials would look the other way. If they weren't forced off the train at the departure station, officials might demand that they disembark along the way.

Jorge and Maria were willing to take that chance. They were lucky at this station. Just as the various officials left the platform, the migrants scrambled to climb the train ladders to the rooftops of the freight cars. Jorge climbed first, followed by Sofia. Maria had noticed Sofia's growing self-confidence, and she watched in amazement as her little girl climbed the ladder readily. When Sofia reached her father, Maria started up the ladder. At five months pregnant, Maria's steps were clumsy; several migrants reached down to help her while Jorge kept a tight hold on Sofia. Maria reached the top just as the train pulled out of the station.

CHAPTER 3

THE BEAST

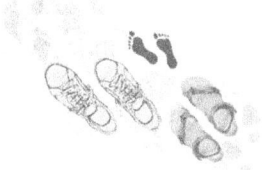

Riding on top of the moving train must be like being on a roller coaster that never ends, Maria thought.

Once migrant families crossed into Mexico, they could head north using one of three options – smugglers, buses, or The Beast, the train the Hernandez family hoped to ride across Mexico. Most of the travelers were fleeing the violence and desperate conditions in Honduras, El Salvador, and Guatemala – and most were poor families with children. Smugglers weren't a viable option; they took extremely dangerous routes not suited for children and, too often, they were unscrupulous. Buses were available but were far too expensive and were often stopped by immigration authorities or gangs from organized crime groups. This left The Beast as the choice made annually by thousands of Central Americans fleeing intolerable circumstances. The Hernandez family had no other option. The Beast was their only hope for traveling across Mexico.

Through the years, there had been very little opposition from public authorities to Central Americans riding The Beast. Then, in 2014, the Mexican government began taking measures designed to *deter migrants from riding the trains. They increased border patrols and checkpoints; railroad companies ordered an increase in the speed of the trains. Authorities hoped to deter the migrants with these measures, but instead, migrants continued to ride The Beast in growing numbers.*

Like so many others who had gone before them, Jorge and Maria remained determined to make this journey on The Beast. Despite the dangers inherent in riding on top of a freight car, they concluded that they had no other choice. Bringing Sofia along, they would board The Beast.

Maria was never as frightened as she was on top of the freight car. She grabbed a railing near Jorge while Sofia clung to her father's neck. As the train departed from the Tapachula station, Maria prayed that they would make it safely to Arriaga, several hours away. The train first lurched forward, then began to gather speed. Maria glanced around her and saw a variety of migrants – men who were alone, some with wives and children, and youths by themselves.

She noticed one young man close to her who smiled at her and said, "Just hold tight. You'll be okay." She noticed that he was carrying a long pole, and she wondered what it was for. Next to him was a woman who reminded Maria of her mother. The woman seemed to be praying while the young man drew her closer to him. Maria asked him if the woman was his mother.

"Yes," the young man replied. "My father was killed by a gang in our village so we left in a hurry. My aunt is in the U.S. and we are going to stay with her. My mother has cancer and my aunt will take care of her. I want to get a job so I can help my family. There's nothing left for us in Honduras.

My name is Carlos. What's yours?"

It was a familiar story, variations of which Maria had heard many times during their trek. She understood the desperation. She and Jorge were equally determined to succeed in starting a new life for themselves and, more importantly, for Sofia and the baby growing in her belly. But now she wondered if riding The Beast was a mistake. She had heard stories about the dangers of riding the trains, especially through southern Mexico. From heart-breaking accounts of migrants falling to their death or losing limbs to kidnapping and rape by organized gangs roaming the train routes, the dangers were overwhelming. Maria tried to dismiss the fear that rose up from deep inside her gut.

Suddenly, she heard yelling toward the front of the freight car. Three men were on their feet, leaning over a family crouched together. Maria saw that one of the men had a knife, and that he appeared to be threatening the family. Maria instinctively crawled over to Jorge and reached for Sofia. Jorge quickly joined Carlos, who had already jumped up, his pole in his hands. Jorge and Carlos approached the three men who were threatening the family. Carlos shouted, "Leave them alone or we will push you off the train."

The man with the knife turned toward them and said with a snarl, "Try to fight us and you are the ones who will die today. We own this train." His two companions stood behind him while the family they were threatening crawled away from the men.

Maria saw her husband glance back at her as if to say, "I have to do this." Carlos swung his pole, caught the leader in his stomach, and sent him flying off the side of the freight car. Maria couldn't believe what she was seeing. Jorge lunged at the second member of the group. They both fell to their knees. Carlos joined Jorge in beating the man until he was bloody.

The third attacker dropped to his knees and begged, "Don't kill me. I was forced to join them!"

"You will get off the train when it stops. Don't argue or you'll be the next to die," Jorge warned.

As if on cue, the train slowed to a stop and the man clamored down the nearest ladder, dragging his injured companion behind him. All the migrants on top of the freight car stood up and clapped, hailing Jorge and Carlos as heroes.

Jorge walked back to Maria and Sofia, collapsed, and said, "They would have tried to make us pay next. We had to fight back." Maria stood up and walked over to Carlos, who had returned to his mother.

"Thank you for being so brave. I will never forget what you did for us," she said. Carlos smiled weakly as he put the pole under his legs so that it wouldn't roll when the train started again. His mother kissed him on his cheek. No one mentioned the man Carlos had pushed off the train. Maria rejoined Jorge and Sofia, comforting her wailing daughter from the distress of witnessing the fight. The train jolted forward, continuing its journey to Arriaga.

Riding on top of the moving train must be like being on a roller coaster that never ends, Maria thought. The freight car rocked back and forth, sometimes so violently that Sofia was knocked off her father's lap. The train sped along as wind whipped the faces of those on top. Pebbles occasionally kicked up from the track causing even greater pain. Maria worried about her unborn child – how could her baby survive the constant jerking around?

Occasionally someone would yell, "Branch!" and everyone bent down to avoid being hit by a tree branch overhang-
ing the train tracks. Worse yet were the deafening sounds of
the train's wheels, which made it impossible for the riders to
talk to each other. Jorge and Maria concentrated on holding
on to the roof railing while, amazingly, Sofia slept with her
arms locked around Jorge's neck.

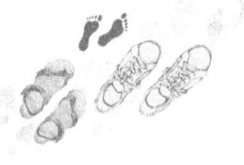

CHAPTER 4

SHELTERED

Jorge counted fifteen individuals and noticed one pair of young men who each had an amputated leg.

The shelter in Arriaga was run out of an old, abandoned Catholic church located near the center of town. It was encircled by an iron fence which offered a measure of security to the migrants who stayed there. As the Hernandez family and the rest of the group approached the gate, a middle-aged man appeared at the front door.

"Welcome, friends," he said with a smile. "I'm Father Miguel. I am the director of this shelter. Would you like to rest here?" The Hernandez family and the rest of the group gratefully accepted the offer and followed the priest into the shelter. Inside the large front room they saw more migrants sitting in chairs and children playing on the floor. There were several fans running and the air was noticeably cooler – a welcome change from the blazing heat outside. Jorge counted fifteen individuals and noticed one pair of young men who each had an amputated leg. To the right of the room was a large opening to the kitchen, where they could see several women preparing meals. Father Miguel showed them to a sunny backroom where cots and mattresses lined the walls and all possible remaining space. He assigned everyone a bed where they gladly deposited their backpacks and duffel bags. Maria sank down on her cot and took off her shoes. She was exhausted, and her feet were badly swollen.

Father Miguel looked at her and then said to the group, "I know you are tired. Why don't you rest before dinner? The rules here are simple. You may stay a total of three nights. We will provide you meals and information. We have only two bathrooms, but there are also sinks outside for washing your face and hands. If you stay more than one night we may ask you to help us with chores around the shelter. We have a nurse who comes every day. She will look at any injuries or problems you may be having. We want you to know that you are safe here and that we will help you."

Jorge took Sofia with him to the front room so that Maria could rest undisturbed. A woman came out of the kitchen and offered cookies to the children. Pitchers with ice water sat on a corner table. Jorge gulped down two large glasses of water and then sat in a chair next to the young men with amputations.

"Hello," Jorge said to the two men. He didn't think it was polite to ask how they lost their legs.

"Welcome," one of the men replied with a smile. "I am Andres and this is Frank. Where are you from?"

Jorge explained how the violence back in his hometown in Honduras forced his family to leave. He shared the threats that gang members made about his wife and how he now worried that her pregnancy would make it difficult for her to reach the border at Reynosa, their destination. In fact, Jorge was more than worried about Maria. The last few weeks of their trek had shown him that Maria was in no shape to continue walking in the blistering heat they were forced to endure every day in Guatemala and Mexico.

Andres listened and looked sadly at Jorge. "There is no safe way to get to the border, my friend. You were lucky to get here on The Beast without losing your legs like we did. Frank and I got caught under the wheels when we tried to get on the slow-moving train. It happened nearby, and we've been in Arriaga for the last three months while we're healing. Father Miguel has been so kind to us. He broke his own rule by letting us stay here until we are well enough to move on."

Jorge was horrified. He thought about the man that Carlos had knocked off the train, then he looked at Sofia playing quietly with a doll she found on a shelf. He could never live with himself if anything happened to his wife or daughter. For a brief moment, he wondered if he should take his family home to Honduras.

Andres continued, "Listen. Frank and I know a man who has agreed to let us ride in his truck to Mexico City. He only wants us to pay for his gas. I trust him and I think you and your family should come with us. We are planning to leave the day after tomorrow."

Jorge said that he would discuss it with Maria. *Perhaps this was the answer to his prayers.*

At dinner, the migrants in the shelter all sat at a long table set up in the front room. Father Miguel said a blessing and everyone eagerly shared heaping plates of tortillas, refried beans, and soup. Maria's rest was welcomed and refreshing; she found herself laughing and crying at the stories fellow travelers shared about their journey north. After dinner they gathered around the priest, who tried to answer their many questions and concerns about what to expect after they left the shelter.

Some of the migrants planned to take the route that led to the border at Tijuana, while others wanted to cross the border at Reynosa. Both routes were dangerous according to Father Miguel. Drug cartels were increasingly brazen in kidnapping migrants for ransom. Brutal rapes and murders were common. It was well-known that Mexican police were corrupt. The Father told a story of one family who was kidnapped by a group of police officers. After robbing them of everything they had, including their clothes, the police threw them into a lake, laughing uproariously as they raced off in patrol cars. A local farmer found the family and brought them to this shelter.

"What happened to that family?' asked Jorge.

"They gave up and went back to their hometown in Honduras." Father Miguel said.

Later, after Sofia fell asleep, Jorge and Maria discussed the offer from Andres and Frank. It seemed like a better option than trying to ride The Beast for the 10 – hour trip to Mexico City. They talked about how trucks were often stopped by gangs or police, but Jorge promised that he would protect his wife and daughter. He said he planned to buy a knife in Arriaga the next day. Maria thought back to how Jorge had protected them from the men on the train; she said, "I am praying that God and my brave husband will keep us safe."

After breakfast the next day Jorge left Maria and Sofia at the shelter, and he walked into town to buy a knife that he hoped he would never have to use. Despite the fact that Arriaga is known as a crossroads for Central American migrants, Jorge felt vulnerable as he walked past Mexican residents glancing at him from their sidewalk café tables. No one smiled and one young girl whispered to her father and pointed at him. Jorge walked into a store that showed farming tools in the window. He walked up to the counter and asked a salesperson if the store carried knives. The employee looked Jorge up and down before he said in a loud voice, "Don't you know that knives are illegal in Mexico?"

Another man in the store approached Jorge. The man had on clean black trousers and a crisp white shirt with traditional embroidery around the edges. Jorge knew that his own faded blue t-shirt and dirty jeans marked him as a migrant. The man came very close to Jorge and snarled, "Why don't you go back where you came from? We don't want your trouble here." Without a word, Jorge quickly left the store and headed further down the street.

Finally, Jorge walked into a store that carried home goods. *Maybe they have knives for cutting meat,* he thought to himself. Fortunately, there was a display of knives next to the pots and pans near the front of the store. He picked out a medium-sized paring knife, paid for it at the check-out counter, and quickly departed. As he walked back to the shelter, he considered his encounter with the Mexican shopper. *Why do the Mexicans hate us? We are all the same, wanting a better life for our children,* he thought. *We need to get to the U.S. soon so we will be safe.* Despite his determined optimism about the future, his anxiety prevailed as Jorge opened the iron gate at the shelter and walked up the steps to reunite with his wife and daughter.

CHAPTER 5

HOPE

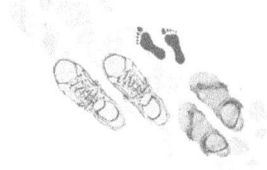

"I hope that I won't have to live in Mexico. I'll never see my family again. Will Trump really do that to us?"

That night, after the women and children had settled on their cots and mattresses, six men gathered around a campfire in the backyard of the church shelter. Frank; Andres; Alberto, a young man traveling alone; Jose, another Honduran who left his family behind; and Mario, an older man from El Salvador, joined Jorge in revealing their physical and mental fatigue, anxiety about the future, and their concern about the days to come. The light illuminated their worn and overwrought faces. Deep sighs and breaks in their voices were audible as they shared their hopes, their fears, and what little information they had about their journeys ahead.

"My uncle is in San Diego. He has a job working in a restaurant and he says I can work there, too," said Alberto. "Maybe I can go to school and learn computer skills. The U.S. will offer many new opportunities."

"Yes, but you have a very long way to go to reach Tijuana first," replied Frank. "We are going to Reynosa, which is not nearly so far. Andres and I will apply for asylum and stay in a shelter until the American police let us cross the border."

"That could take years!" exclaimed Mario.

"I don't think so," replied Jorge. "I've heard that the shelters on the Texas borders are so crowded that the authorities are letting us go in the streets of McAllen, Texas."

"Maybe, but Trump has a new policy called *Remain in Mexico*," added Jose as he poked at the fire. "I joined a caravan after I testified against some robbers back in Honduras in 2012. Then, last year, the government let them out of prison. The government had promised me protection but it didn't happen. The robbers knew where I lived and they left notes telling my mother and my wife to prepare for my death. I had to leave. I hope that I won't have to live in Mexico. I'll never see my family again. Will Trump really do that to us?"

Frank stepped closer to the fire and handed one of his crutches to Andres. He warmed his hands close to the flames and said, "The American people won't let us stay in Mexico's shelters forever even if Trump wants us to. Americans have a Constitution and I've heard that lawyers are saying that keeping us out of the U.S. in dangerous shelters is unconstitutional."

Andres nodded. "Even if we stay in Reynosa for a long time, it will be better than going back to Honduras."

Frank turned toward Alberto. "The shelters in Tijuana are very crowded and violent," he stated emphatically. "I heard that two young men from Honduras were robbed and murdered there last year. You should think about coming to Reynosa with us in the morning."

Alberto shook his head. "I can take care of myself," he said. "I want to live and work with my uncle. He is the only family I have left." With that declaration, Alberto settled on the ground closer to the fire and donned his headphones. The bass rhythm of the American pop music Alberto loved could be heard and prompted the other men to tap their feet and, for a moment, think of more joyful times.

Following that brief exchange, Jorge asked the question that had been on his mind for days. "What about hiring a coyote to help us get across the border? My wife is now six months pregnant, and my daughter is only five years old. Isn't getting across the Rio Grande better than rotting in a shelter for who knows how long?"

There was a long pause. Finally, Mario spoke up. "I didn't want to say anything, but I have a guy who is going to get me across the border to Texas. I am traveling with my wife and two grandchildren. My daughter and her husband were murdered by the MS-13 gang in El Salvador. They have threatened me, too. They say that if I don't pay them, they will kill my grandchildren." Mario wiped his eyes and continued, "It costs $5,000 for this smuggler to get us over the border. It is all the money I have saved; my cousins also gave me money to save our lives. I know it's dangerous but my wife and I want our grandchildren to have a better life. I don't think we will all be safe if we stay in Reynosa. The MS-13 gang members will be looking for us."

For a while, the crisp air was filled with wafting smoke and complete silence. Then Frank spoke, choosing his words carefully. "I have heard many terrible stories about these coyotes. Most do not care at all about the migrants they're smuggling; some have suffocated in overcrowded trucks and others have died in the desert. The coyotes have kidnapped the women, raping and brutalizing them, and using them later for ransom. Do you trust this smuggler?"

Mario replied, "I met this guy in El Salvador. He knew some people in my town and they introduced me to him. We talked for a long time while I was sizing him up. I could tell that he had a lot of experience getting migrants across the border. He said he is not a member of the drug cartel, but that he does work as a team with a couple of other coyotes. He knows about the border walls, the habits of the American police, and how to keep us from being noticed. He said he has done this for ten years and has gotten hundreds of people into the U.S. He knows all the best places to cross the Rio Grande."

Addressing all of the men around the fire, Jorge said, "God will keep us safe. We will pray for you, Mario, and your family. The worst that can happen is that you will be deported back to Honduras. Then you try again, right?"

Mario sighed and said, "I don't know if we could do this again. My wife is terrified, and my grandchildren have bad colds. We saw the nurse today at the shelter, and she gave us some medicine and bandages for our feet. So, we will walk and get rides north until we meet up with the coyote."

It seemed to Jorge that these men and their families had suffered greatly. He thought about the suffering his family had endured through this part of their journey; he hated seeing Maria and his precious daughter worn down and uncomfortable. It was hard enough for him to witness Sofia get a splinter in her tiny hand or a blister on her foot. He knew, though, that the real challenges and suffering were yet to come. Jorge didn't have $5,000; he was the only means of support his family had. He felt the paring knife in his pocket and thought, *No knife can protect us against the drug cartel's gangs. The only one on Earth who can take care of my family is me.*

By this time, the campfire had dwindled down to glowing embers, and the men were getting chilly. Jorge confirmed with Frank and Andres that they would meet in the front room at 5 am. He then turned to Alberto, who was humming to the music in his ears, eyes closed. Jorge tapped him on the shoulder. Alberto looked up at Jorge, who said, "We're going inside now. You're going to get sick if you stay out here."

Alberto replied, "I'll be fine. I like it out here."

Jorge shook his head and commiserated with Frank and Andres, "It's hard to talk any sense into these young people." Five of the men walked together back into the shelter.

CHAPTER 6

THE ROAD

The driver handed a fistful of money to the officer, who quickly counted the amount. "I think this woman is worth more than this!" the officer shouted.

At 5 am the next morning, Maria roused Sofia from her sleep. "Wake up, my little princess," she said quietly. "We are leaving for Mexico City this morning."

The last few days at the shelter in Arriaga were a welcome rest for Maria. For the first time in weeks, she ate something other than beans and tortillas. She rested with her feet up while Sofia played with the other children in the shelter. Most importantly, she was able to sleep without having nightmares. Her experience on top of the train had shaken her, both literally and figuratively. Maria couldn't erase the image of Carlos pushing their attacker off the train from her collection of other traumatic memories. Now, she was planning to ride in the back of a truck for ten hours to Mexico City? What kinds of dangers would she, Jorge, and Sofia encounter during this portion of their trek? She had heard stories of kidnappings, rape, and bribery of corrupt police in exchange for safe passage. Just the thought of any harm coming to Sofia or her unborn child made Maria start to shake. *Would God protect them from these evils in Mexico?*

The three of them joined Andres and Frank in the front room of the shelter to say goodbye to Father Miguel, who offered a touching prayer for their safety. He handed them each a bottle of water and said, "Go with God" as they left the shelter. The early morning was still dark and the air was chilly; Maria buttoned up Sofia's hoodie and pulled her own jacket over her growing belly. She then took her daughter's hand, and they all began walking toward the edge of town. Their progress was slow, but their spirits were high as Andres and Frank limped along on their crutches, softly singing a lively tune. Andres, in particular, was all smiles as he whispered his hopes to Jorge.

"What are you going to do when you get to the States, Jorge?" he asked. "I can't wait to get a new leg and start living a normal life. I want to work in a hospital and help others; maybe even study to become a health aide."

For a few moments, Jorge didn't respond as he considered the future. "I just want my family to be safe. I don't care what I do as long as I don't have to worry about Maria, Sofia, and the baby," he finally said.

Andres smiled again and reminded Jorge of the good news that had motivated them to trek to the U.S. in the first place. "You will be safe in the U.S. Just think about all the wonderful things you'll be able to do. You're a healthy, young man! Many businesses need help. Sofia will go to a good school and Maria will have a great big, healthy son!"

"Now that IS a dream, isn't it?" replied Jorge. "Another healthy baby girl would be a blessing from God, too," he added.

The group reached the edge of town just as the sunrise began to brighten the beautiful blue sky. They waited at an intersection of two dirt roads that seemed to lead nowhere. It wasn't long before an old, dilapidated flatbed truck with wooden sideboards approached them, just as Frank had arranged. Two men stepped out of the truck and approached Andres for payment of gas expenses. Andres handed a wad of bills to the truck driver without a word. The driver counted the bills and instructed the group to climb aboard the flatbed. The truck was almost filled with boxes and crates of vegetables - tomatoes, tomatillos, avocados, *chayote*,[4] and peppers. Jorge climbed onto the flatbed first, then helped Maria. He told her to find a place near the cab window, where she and Sofia wouldn't be spotted easily. Next, Jorge mustered all his strength to help Andres and Frank onto the flatbed. This wasn't an easy task given the men's disabilities, but Jorge assisted them hurriedly to minimize the risk of being stopped before they started their long journey. When everyone was settled, Jorge secured the rear gate of the truck. Within just a couple of minutes, the truck left Arriaga and began the arduous journey to Mexico City.

For the most part, the first half of the trip was uneventful. The truck drivers told the group to help themselves to fresh vegetables when they got hungry. They even gave Sofia a bag of *Beny Locochas Chamoy*, her favorite candy. The first time Maria tapped on the truck's back window to signal the need to stop, the driver was irritated. His attitude changed, however, when he realized her condition. Now in her sixth

---

4 An edible plant known for its versatility and texture rather than its bland taste.

month of pregnancy, Maria needed stops at least every two hours. She had grown accustomed to relieving herself on the side of the road from the walk with the caravan in Guatemala, but Mexico was different. Here, the roads were busy and filled with trucks of all kinds - many of the smaller ones carrying migrants. Jorge worried every time the truck stopped that the police would see them. That could only mean trouble. Their truck drivers anticipated this possibility, however, and stopped only in locations where other vehicles were stopped, such as at gas stations and food stands.

Their luck ran out, however, a few hundred miles south of Mexico City. Out of nowhere, a Mexican police car pulled up alongside the truck and signaled for it to pull over. The group of migrants immediately dropped to the floor of the flatbed, hoping not to be noticed. The two officers approached the truck driver.

"Papers, please," demanded one officer. "Where are you coming from?" he asked.

"Arriaga, sir. We are going to Mexico City to sell our vegetables," the driver replied, trying to sound matter-of-fact.

The second officer walked slowly around the truck. Just as he walked back to the driver's door, Sofia blurted out, "Mama, are we there?"

Both officers rushed to the back of the truck and shouted, "Everyone off! Now!" Jorge helped Andres and Frank with their crutches and the three men climbed out of the back of the truck.

The two officers looked at each other and laughed. "Well, if this isn't a great-looking bunch of migrants! Do you think you will make it across the border?" One of the officers smirked, "that is a joke!"

The other officer added, "I heard a child. Everyone must get out of the truck."

Maria and Sofia climbed out and went over to stand next to Jorge on the side of the road. One of the officers then held Jorge's arms while the other shoved his hands up Maria's blouse.

He looked at Jorge, grinning, and said, "Maybe she is smuggling drugs. One never knows what one will find." Jorge struggled unsuccessfully to get loose while tears streamed down Maria's cheeks.

At that moment, both of the truck drivers got out of the cab and walked over to the officers. "Officer," one driver said. "What do you want from us?"

The officer who was touching Maria responded. "What can you offer?"

The driver handed a fistful of money to the officer, who quickly counted the amount. "I think this woman is worth more than this!" the officer shouted.

The second driver handed the officer more money. The corrupt officer of the law then said pleasantly, as if oblivious to the terror he had just brought upon Maria, "You can all get back into the truck as we have not found any contraband. Have a pleasant journey."

The officer holding Jorge released him and sauntered with his partner back to their police car. As the car sped off, Jorge ran to Maria and held her close.

"Why is Mommy crying?" asked Sofia.

Chapter 7

Kindness

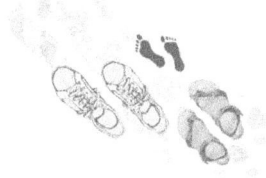

Hundreds, maybe thousands, of migrants were gathered on the field - some lying down on blankets, others walking around.

Jorge helped Andres and Frank climb back into the truck after their traumatic encounter with the Mexican police. Maria and Sofia followed and went back to their previous hiding spot near the cab window. "What should I give to our drivers to help pay for the bribe they paid the officers?" Jorge asked Andres.

Surprisingly, Andres responded with a dismissive wave. "You're welcome to contribute what you are able to pay, Jorge. But these drivers were prepared for this; it wasn't a surprise. They have been helping migrants go north for years. They make a lot of money from smuggling. As soon as they drop you off in Mexico City at the stadium, they will sell their load of vegetables to the agencies feeding the migrants there. Then, they will start recruiting migrants for smuggling at the border. Do you want to hire them to guide you across the border?"

Jorge was taken aback. He thought the truck drivers were really vegetable farmers. "I'm sure it costs more than I have," Jorge said. "Do you know how much they will charge?"

"Well, depending on where they take you, it will cost many thousands of dollars. Plus, I don't think they will want to include Sofia," Frank added. "Children slow down their parents and make it almost impossible for coyotes to be successful in what they are hired to do."

Jorge responded firmly, "I will never leave Maria and Sofia."

"We thought that would be the case. That's why we didn't bring it up earlier, Jorge," Andres said. "Our drivers will take your family to the stadium, where there are many hundreds of migrant families like yours. Frank and I will continue north in this truck and hope that these coyotes will get us across the border."

As he listened to Andres, Jorge realized how fortunate he was to have met the two men. They were good men who had proven to be good friends to his family. He bowed his head and said a quick prayer of thanks to God for this blessing. "Thank you for your help," he said simply to Andres and Frank. Jorge walked back to where Maria and Sofia sat and told his wife what he had learned.

Nothing had prepared Maria for the fear she felt at the hands of the officer who had groped her and his partner who had restrained Jorge, preventing him from helping her. Now, upon hearing that this kind of behavior by Mexican police was expected, she exploded with indignation. "How dare the police disrespect women like that!" she exclaimed. "How can the Mexican government allow this?"

Jorge was unnerved by Maria's naiveté; he realized it was

long overdue to educate his wife about the dangers in their path. He still had not told her about the threats of rape made against her by gangs back home in Honduras, nor had he shared the stories he had heard about migrant women who were kidnapped and sexually abused while traveling through Mexico. Speaking low into Maria's ear so that Sofia couldn't hear him, Jorge explained that many migrant women were abused and even murdered in their attempts to reach the U.S. border.

Maria didn't say anything as she listened to Jorge. But for the next few hours, as the truck grew closer to Mexico City, she pondered his words. She realized that she had a lot to learn about life outside of her town in Honduras. Her family lived much like families lived for generations before her in Honduras - until the gangs changed everything. Even when her brother was murdered, Maria felt relatively safe in the bosom of her family. Women in her culture did not get involved in much outside the home. They might help by getting work where they could, but that usually involved very low wage jobs such as house cleaning or helping out in *cantinas*[5] as they were able. Since most women had little education, they also lacked knowledge about the causes of poverty, drugs, violence, or government corruption. Women like Maria counted on their fathers and husbands to make decisions and keep them safe.

Maria's experience with the Mexican police officer was a wake-up call for her – a sudden jolt into the reality of her circumstances, with or without Jorge by her side in the grueling trek. She knew that what lay ahead in their journey could be even more dangerous. For the first time, Maria

5 Casual restaurant, bar, or wine shop.

made a conscious decision to do everything in her power to take care of herself, her daughter, and her unborn child. *If something were to happen to Jorge*, Maria thought, *I will have to be the strong one.* She sat in the back of the rickety old truck considering all she'd concluded just minutes ago, stroking Sofia's hair as her child slept peacefully – oblivious to all the challenges her mother faced. Maria bowed her head and asked God for wisdom, strength, peace, and resolve during the days ahead.

The *Jesus Martinez Stadium* in Mexico City was a beehive of activity. After the truck pulled up to the entrance of the stadium, Jorge got off first and thanked the drivers, Andres, and Frank for everything they had done to help him and his family. He, Maria, and Sofia followed the crowd going inside the stadium, where they saw an astounding scene. Hundreds, maybe thousands, of migrants were gathered on the field – some lying down on blankets, others walking around. Many of them were women with children; mothers looked harried as they tried to keep their children within sight. Maria gripped Sofia's hand tightly as she glanced around the crowd. She noticed tables set up in various places where people were serving food. Jorge spotted a table where blankets and warm clothing for the women and children were being distributed. The Hernandez family made their way over to that table where they were greeted warmly, given provisions, and told to find a spot to rest in an area that had not yet filled up. Women and children were instructed to sleep at night in a tented area of the stadium, while men had to sleep outside on the field or on the bleachers. After the family's experience with the police, Maria and Jorge were heartened to feel welcomed – at least here in the stadium.

It was much cooler here than in the southern regions of Mexico, and Maria was grateful to have warmer clothing. After a light dinner meal of soup and tortillas, she and Sofia found a cot under one of the stadium tents. That night, Maria started a conversation with another young Honduran mother in the cot next to hers. The woman, Alma, shared her own harrowing story of personal experiences on the road. She and her 10-year old daughter had left Honduras after her husband was murdered. She joined a caravan and walked north with hundreds of other migrants. At one point when they were walking through Chiapas, her daughter became ill, and they had to drop out of the caravan. While they rested near the highway, a car full of men saw them, stopped, and dragged them into a nearby field. Alma was raped repeatedly, while her terrified daughter was forced to watch.

Alma, bruised and in shock, walked with her daughter to a nearby farm, where the family kindly took care of them for a few days. The family arranged for Alma and her daughter to ride with a neighbor to Mexico City. Fortunately, he was kind and meant them no harm; he dropped them off here at the stadium. Alma also warned Maria that the assault was not unusual for vulnerable migrant women. She had prepared for this possibility by taking a birth control injection in Honduras before starting her journey. Once again, Maria was stunned at what she was hearing about the dangers for women trying to reach to the U.S. border.

The next day, the family showered at an area of the stadium set up for personal washing. There was even an area for washing clothes, where a volunteer from Catholic Charities offered clean t-shirts donated from churches in the U.S. to the migrants. Maria was relieved to wash their sweaty and dirty clothes after her family's long truck ride in the hot sun of Mexico. She contemplated this generosity and hoped that one day, she, too, would be prosperous in North America and able to donate to others in need. *Americans must be kind people*, Maria concluded.

The next stop was the medical station where a nurse made sure Maria's unborn baby was still thriving. She also gave Sofia a lollipop, which was all the little girl needed to transform her frown into a big grin. A relieved Maria and a happy Sofia rejoined Jorge, who, in his conversations with other migrants, had gathered a lot of information to help them plan how they would travel from the stadium to the Texas border.

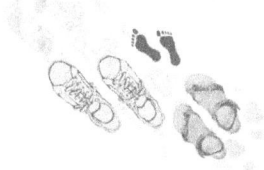

CHAPTER 8

DECISIONS

I don't think we can trust the Mexican government. They are doing this only because U.S. President Trump doesn't want us. He thinks we are rapists and terrorists.

While Maria talked with other women at night under the stadium tents, Jorge likewise conversed with other men, learning important news and information from those who were hoping to reach the border. Every night that Jorge spread a blanket on the stadium bleachers, he had the opportunity to talk with others nearby. Hundreds of men like himself were making decisions about how to achieve their dreams. Many of the men were alone, leaving family behind in Central America. Their goals were to find work, and they were willing to do almost anything to get into Texas, Arizona, New Mexico, or California.

Their stories were not new. For decades, men from Mexico and further south had entered the U.S., both legally and illegally. Jorge knew that some villages in Honduras and Guatemala were almost entirely supported by the money sent from these men back to their families at home. Some families lived quite well in nice homes in towns that no longer had a self-sustaining economy. What was different now were the increased numbers of Hondurans fleeing their homes. Jorge learned from his conversations that hundreds of migrants now requested asylum every day at the U.S. border.

Other men in the stadium had their families with them, like Jorge. The sheer determination and grit of these families both astounded and inspired Jorge. He met one man whose wife and four children, ages 3–10, walked with him for weeks from southern Honduras. They faced hunger, sickness, and exhaustion every day, yet they never gave up. The man explained to Jorge that he had no choice – he had no job opportunities and the gangs took all his money. He also added that if he and his family did return to their home, they would almost certainly all be murdered.

While Jorge and his family were in the stadium, news spread among the migrants about a new program available to them in Mexico. Mexican President Enrique Pena Nieto, commonly called EPN, had launched a program called *You Are Home*, which promised shelter, medical attention, schooling, and jobs to Central Americans who agreed to stay in the southern Mexico states of Chiapas or Oaxaca, far from the U.S. border. Most of the migrants Jorge talked with in the stadium seemed determined to reach the U.S., despite the offer of refuge. However, he noted that pregnant women, children, and the elderly were especially encouraged to join the program. Many of these vulnerable migrants seemed to be taking up EPN's offer and were now traveling back to the shelters.

As Jorge and Maria watched Sofia play with other children in a big sandbox, Jorge turned to Maria and asked,

⊷ 56 ⊷

"Should we join this program, *You Are Home?* I want you and Sofia to be safe – and terrible things could happen during the rest of our journey."

Maria thought for a moment. This program could be the answer to her prayers. But she remembered the promise she made to herself – she would be strong for her family. She no longer wanted to depend on others to take care of her and her children. "I don't think we can trust the Mexican government. They are doing this only because U.S. President Trump doesn't want us. He thinks we are rapists and terrorists. As soon as Trump looks away, EPN will send us back to Honduras. That's why the program requires us to live in Chiapas."

Jorge was impressed with his wife's analysis. He was also surprised. Maria had always depended on him to make decisions for their family. Overnight, she appeared to be more assertive than in the past. He wondered what caused her new-found self-confidence. Whatever the reason, he was happy to share the burden of family responsibility for decision-making. He loved his wife and they had been through a lot together. They needed to be a strong team to get across the border; he feared it would be anything but easy.

"I think you are right, my love," Jorge responded. "We should continue with our dream of starting a new life in North America. I heard from the other men that there will be many buses here at the stadium in the morning," Jorge said. "Those who signed up for *You Are Home* will be bussed south to Chiapas. There will be buses going to Reynosa and a few will start the long drive west to Tijuana. Do you still want to go to Reynosa?"

Maria didn't hesitate in her reply. "Yes, it's a shorter

drive and I am anxious to get across the border so that our new baby will be born in the U.S. They can't deny us asylum, right? The gangs threatened us and killed my brother!"

Jorge shrugged his shoulders and said, "According to what I've heard, Trump is trying to make it difficult for people who are fleeing gang violence. Every day, the rules change. Not only that, but we have to apply for asylum status and then wait to see an official. The wait could take months. What I'm not sure about is whether we wait in the U.S. or in Mexico. There are Catholic shelters in Reynosa and U.S. Border Patrol Respite Houses in McAllen. I don't think where our baby is born is up to us. Even if our baby is born in the U.S., Trump is trying to change the laws granting birthright citizenship."

This news was very disturbing to Maria but she was determined to appear strong and optimistic for Jorge's benefit. "We just have to deal with things day by day, don't we? God will guide us and, eventually, we will live in the U.S. We have to keep trying, Jorge. We have to do this for Sofia and the new baby. By the way, Jorge, do you think our new baby will be a boy or girl? I know you want a boy but I want Sofia to have a sister. They will need each other to deal with all the suffering that awaits them in this world."

Jorge regarded Maria's words as an attempt to lighten the conversation but Jorge wasn't fooled. He took Maria into his arms and held her tightly. "Maria, God will make sure our children have a much better life than we have had. I will fight for their future as long as I live. Even if we have to stay in Mexico, it's better than Honduras. We have each other and we will always be a family. Yes, I'd like a son, but another baby girl would be a blessing, too. If the baby is a boy, I'd like to name him Miguel, to honor both your brother and Father Miguel. If it is a girl, what name do you like?"

Maria couldn't stop the tears forming as she said, "I would like to name our second daughter Alicia. It's a beautiful name that's popular in North America and in Honduras."

Jorge placed his hand on Maria's baby bump and whispered into her ear, "I can't wait to meet either Miguel or Alicia. I love you, Maria."

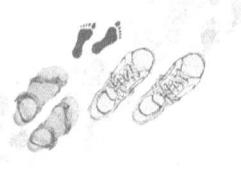

CHAPTER 9

KIDNAPPED!

As he shoved Maria ahead of him to the front of the bus, the second attacker kicked Jorge and yelled, 'This will teach you that Los Zetas is the boss in Mexico!"

The buses were lined up by 7 AM in front of the stadium. There must have been twenty of them, and they were the biggest, fanciest buses that Maria had ever seen. Migrants milled around in the parking lot, talking and laughing, looking for all the world like a crowd of tourists getting ready to go sight-seeing. Maria thought the whole scene was surreal. She wasn't laughing. She knew that the buses were taking the migrants to their destinies. *Board the wrong bus and one could end up back in Arriaga. Get on the right bus and head for uncertainty at the border.*

As if to echo her mother's intense thoughts, Sofia looked up in five-year old confusion, squinting in the morning sunlight, "Mommy, which bus are we getting on?"

Maria smiled down at her daughter and replied, "We are getting on the bus that will take us to the border with the U.S. Won't that be wonderful?"

"Can we get on the bus with Giselle and Javier, Mommy? They are my friends and we want to play together on the bus." Sofia's innocence made Maria smile.

"We'll have to see if their families are going where we are going," Maria replied to her daughter.

While Maria and Sofia waited in line for instructions regarding which bus to board, Jorge was talking with other migrants across the parking lot. Maria had come to expect Jorge to be the source of all the latest information. He was more gregarious than Maria, and he enjoyed meeting new people. Maria preferred to observe what was happening around her rather than trust the words of a stranger.

When an official announced which buses were going to Reynosa, Maria yelled to Jorge, "Hurry up, Jorge, or you will end up staying in Mexico!"

He rushed over to his family and they boarded the bus for what they expected to be the last leg of their journey to a new and better life. They found empty seats near the back of the bus. Sofia squealed in delight as she discovered that her friends, Giselle and Javier, were sitting with their families close by.

Once they were settled, Jorge told Maria that there was uncertainty as to who sponsored the buses loading migrants from the stadium. Some migrants said the Mexican federal government chartered the buses. Others said they heard the Mexico City government was anxious for the migrants to leave and bypassed the federal government. Still other migrants maintained that several caravan leaders negotiated with major charities, including the Catholic Church, to provide this transportation. What was important to Jorge was the reassurance that the buses were not run by the drug cartels.

Two bus drivers would share driving duties to cover the 600 miles between Mexico City and Reynosa; the bus would stop approximately every two hours for restroom and food breaks. In total, the drivers said the trip would take two days. Maria noticed that she was the only obviously pregnant passenger on their bus, but there was a handful of families with children. She tried to relax as the bus left the stadium and began its long journey north.

The first bathroom and food stop couldn't come soon enough for Maria. She noted other buses parked and migrants headed for the restrooms. When the women who were waiting in the restroom line saw Maria's baby bump, many waved her and Sofia to the front of the line. Maria was grateful for their acknowledgement of her needs. One woman offered to watch Sofia while Maria attended to herself. She thought to herself, *Becoming pregnant is like joining a club. Women know what it's like and we take care of each other.* It was one of the few comforting thoughts Maria had experienced in the last several weeks. It would certainly be her last for many days ahead.

It was pitch black at 2 AM, and the bus passengers were fast asleep when it happened. Suddenly, the bus slowed down and pulled over to the side of the road. Within seconds, two men with guns burst through the door and screamed for everyone to put their hands over their heads. Dressed in black clothing with scarves tied around their faces, the criminals revealed no clues as to their identities. It wouldn't have made much difference if they could have been identified, since they were so often in cahoots with corrupt police. By the time the children started crying, the men had already dragged the two bus drivers off the bus. They quickly returned, pointing their guns at first one side of the aisle, then the other, advancing rapidly toward the back of the bus. The first attacker seemed to be in charge as he barked orders to his accomplice. "Take this one," he shouted, as he pointed his gun into the chest of a young man near the front of the bus. His partner grabbed the young man and dragged him off the bus.

"Everyone on this bus - silent! Do as I say and keep your hands up!" the first man shouted as he waved his gun from one side of the bus to the other.

When the second man returned, the two men walked past several more rows of seats before the first man stopped again. The next victim was a young woman Maria had gotten to know at the stadium. She had traveled from Guatemala with a caravan, leaving her family behind to care for her parents. She screamed as she was dragged from the bus and the second man hit her hard across her face.

Sofia cried to Maria, "Mommy, Mommy, what is happening? "

Jorge was trying to keep Sofia quiet when the first attacker strode up to the three of them. "Well, well. What a nice family." He pointed his gun directly at Jorge and glanced at Maria, who was trying to cover her belly with the squirming Sofia. "A pretty wife and another child on the way," he said with a sneer, "I bet you would pay dearly for your wife, wouldn't you?"

Instantly, Jorge reacted. He jumped up from his seat and hit the man in his stomach as hard as he could. As the man doubled over, the other attacker pointed his own gun at Jorge and shot him, hitting Jorge in his shoulder. Jorge fell to the dirty bus floor as chaos erupted all around him.

The first attacker stood up and grabbed Maria from her seat, leaving Sofia wailing while Jorge was struggling to get up. As he shoved Maria ahead of him to the front of the bus, the second attacker kicked Jorge and yelled, "This will teach you that Los Zetas is the boss in Mexico!"

When Maria was pushed out of the bus door, she saw three more men standing in front of her on the side of the road. One man pointed a gun at the bus drivers. The other two restrained the hostages. Maria's kidnapper pushed her over to the group and then instructed the two drivers to get back on the bus and drive away quickly.

As the drivers dashed up the steps to the bus, the man who grabbed Maria yelled at them with a laugh. "Have a pleasant trip to the border!" Uproarious laughter from all the kidnappers followed.

Maria watched with horror as the scene unfolded. She was in a state of shock and couldn't get a sound out of her mouth as she watched the bus – with her husband and child on board - leaving without her. Instinctively, Maria's hand went to her belly.

CHAPTER 10

CARTEL

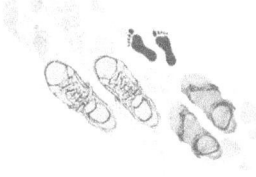

What if the kidnappers called him and wanted a ransom?
He had very little money. What if it wasn't enough?

The birth of Mexico's major cartels can be traced to Miguel Ángel Félix Gallardo, "The Godfather," who in the 1980s partnered with Colombian cocaine trafficker Pablo Escobar of the infamous Medellin cartel. After Felix Gallardo was arrested in 1989, he divided up the drug trade he controlled among relatives and powerful families, who then began fighting for dominance. He left the Gulf Cartel undisturbed under its original founder, Osiel Cardenas Guillen. There was a lull in the fighting among the various drug cartels during the late 1990s but the violence has steadily worsened since 2000.

In 1999, Cardenas Guillen hired a group of corrupt former elite military soldiers to work for him. These former Special Forces soldiers became known as Los Zetas and began operating as a private army for the Gulf Cartel. During the early 2000s the Zetas were instrumental in the Gulf Cartel's domination of the drug trade in much of Mexico. Many factors have contributed to the escalating violence *over the last twenty years. One important reason was the unraveling of a longtime implicit arrangement between narcotics traffickers and Mexican government administrations. Beginning in the late 1980s, Mexican presidents implemented various military actions to combat the cartels, but this failed to significantly reduce the growing rates of homicides and kidnappings.*

In 2013 Mexico saw the rise of the controversial para-military groups led by land-owners, ranchers, and other rural businessmen. These local groups fought against criminals that wanted to impose dominance in their towns. The Mexican government's initial support for these groups crumbled when the para-military groups were infiltrated by criminal elements. This made it impossible to distinguish between civilian militia convoys and drug-cartel convoys. In addition, Mexican President Enrique Pena's handling of the 2014 Iguala mass kidnapping and the 2015 escape of drug lord "El Chapo" Guzmán from the Altiplano maximum security prison prompted international criticism.

In recent years, cartels have diversified well beyond their drug trafficking. The thousands of migrants from Central America who travel through Mexico are easy prey for gangs associated with drug cartels. The gangs smuggle migrants across the border with the U.S. and, increasingly, they extort migrants from caravans, trucks, and buses.

For the cartels, the biggest moneymaker is a toll fee, or "piso," that criminals force migrants to pay to continue traveling. The criminals also kidnap and hold them until the victims' family members pay a ransom. They may compel the migrants to cultivate cartel marijuana or poppy fields, or simply rob and brutalize them. Others are compelled to act as "mules" to smuggle drugs such as marijuana stuffed inside backpacks or "mochilas," a type of bag commonly used in Central America.

As soon as the masked gunman left the bus with Maria and the two other hostages, several bus passengers ran to Jorge's aid. One man took off his shirt and wrapped it around Jorge's shoulder, trying to stop the profuse bleeding.

Another said she would call the police. A third made her way to Sofia, who was twisting the tear-soaked hem of her t-shirt at her cheek screaming, "Mommy! Mommy! They have my mommy!"

"No! Don't call the police. They won't do anything and Maria will be in worse danger," Jorge pleaded. Several others agreed with him.

Seconds later, the two drivers were back on the bus. One returned to the driver's seat and quickly maneuvered the bus back onto the highway. The other sat on the floor next to him, still shaken from their brief, but traumatic experience. The entire incident had lasted only a few minutes. Of the three migrants who were kidnapped, only Maria had family members on the bus. Sofia - rejecting the kind offer of comfort and crying louder still - asked Jorge, "Where's Mommy? Will we go back to get her, Daddy?"

Jorge tried to comfort his daughter while reaching for his cell phone. He knew it was only a matter of time before he would receive a call from the kidnappers, demanding a ransom for Maria. While he sat with Sofia, another migrant ran up to the front of the bus.

"We have an injured man in the back of the bus. You must drive the bus to the closest hospital," the migrant urgently exclaimed to the bus driver.

The two drivers looked at each other. The one on the floor replied, "How bad is he injured? We are only a couple of hours from Reynosa. It would be better for all of us if we drive there. We can trust the doctors and police in Reynosa."

Jorge and the other migrants understood this reasoning. They knew that this part of Mexico was very dangerous and few medical facilities were nearby. So, for the remainder of the bus trip, passengers tended to Jorge and Sofia with gentleness and compassion. They alternated between applying pressure to Jorge's shoulder to stop the bleeding and offering solace to Sofia. The driver seated on the floor used his phone to call the shelter in Reynosa run by Catholic Charities. The shelter's director reassured him that medical help would be available as soon as the bus arrived.

Jorge used those remaining hours on the bus to think about his predicament. For Sofia's sake, he controlled his emotions and focused on reassuring her that her mother would be with them again soon. The reality was that he wasn't sure of anything. Mostly, he was angry with himself for not adequately protecting Maria. If only he had stabbed the kidnapper with the knife in his back pocket. Maybe that would have scared the second man away. Now, he was overwhelmed with fear for his wife. And what about the baby? Jorge felt his stomach jump into his throat, despite the pain from his shoulder wound.

So many "what ifs" crowded Jorge's thoughts. *What if the kidnappers called him and wanted a ransom? He had very little money. What if it wasn't enough? What if the kidnappers murdered his beloved Maria?* Jorge felt tears well up but he quickly wiped his eyes. He couldn't let Sofia sense his fear.

At last, the bus pulled up to the door of the Catholic shelter in Reynosa. The other passengers waited to let Jorge and Sofia disembark first. Two police officers met them and took a quick look at Jorge's wound. Sister Edna, shelter director, bent down to Sofia and gently took her hand. "Hello, Sofia. Your daddy is going to the hospital to see a doctor. He will be back soon. You will stay here with me to wait for him. I have breakfast for you and a puppy who wants to play with you."

Sofia turned to Jorge. "Daddy, will you come back soon?'

Jorge leaned down to his daughter and hugged her as best he could, wincing in pain from his shoulder wound. "I will be back very soon, my sweet Sofia. I love you. Now, go eat breakfast and be a good girl while I'm gone."

Jorge had a hard time letting go of his daughter. Just as he gently freed her, a puppy ran up to Sofia, its tail wagging furiously. It was just what Sofia needed. Jorge turned away, tears in his eyes. He and the two officers got into the police car and headed for Reynosa General Hospital.

Chapter 11

Assault

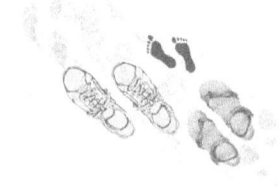

In her anguished thoughts, she prayed: Please God, make it end. Please, God.

As soon as the bus sped away, the kidnappers dragged the three hostages over to their pick-up truck. Maria was the last to climb into the back of the truck. One captor pushed her roughly and yelled loudly, "Hurry up, Mommy!"

Maria scrambled to the outstretched hands of the other woman and sat next to her on the bare metal truck bed. They were all too frightened to speak as three kidnappers positioned themselves around the migrants. The remaining two men got into the cab and started the truck. One kidnapper kept his gun pointed at Maria and the other two hostages as the truck turned back onto the highway.

Once she caught her breath, Maria forced herself to consider the reality of her situation. She was six months pregnant and she had just been kidnapped by a gang of men from a drug cartel. Her husband was shot and she didn't know how seriously he was wounded. She and the other two hostages had no way to escape, and she had no idea where they were being taken. Worst of all, she worried about Sofia. *Who would take care of her if Jorge was injured? What if Jorge died?* The thought of losing her husband was almost more than she could bear but, for the first time in her life, she made a conscious decision to get control of herself and talk herself through her options.

I have to escape. They will kill me and my baby if I don't, Maria determined silently, even though she had no idea how she would get away from these horrible men...these hardened criminals. She knew they would kill all three of their hostages without any hesitation if they didn't get what they wanted. She also knew that what the kidnappers wanted above anything else was undoubtedly getting a huge ransom for her. Without a paid ransom, she and her unborn child were in grave danger. Even if Jorge somehow raised enough money to offer it, she had heard that migrants were often murdered anyway. Her only hope was to escape.

By this time, all three of the kidnappers had removed their face scarves and were talking with each other. Maria turned toward the two other hostages sitting beside her in the truck and whispered, "What are your names?"

"Isabella," the young woman replied, her voice low and shaky.

"Carlos," the young male offered, equally as unnerved as Isabella.

"We must help each other survive whatever happens. I will think of some way for us to escape," Maria promised the other two migrants.

At this point, one of the kidnappers turned back toward the migrants and said menacingly, "No talking if you want to live another day." He looked at Maria's belly and added, "Don't think that being pregnant will give you any special treatment." The man leered at Maria, exposing a mouth with only a few teeth. Maria noticed that one side of his face bore a long scar. She thought he was the ugliest, scariest man she had ever seen. He turned back to his compatriots and muttered something that Maria couldn't hear. All three of the men looked at Maria and roared with laughter.

Isabella squeezed Maria's hand; Maria knew they would help one another through whatever awaited them. Carlos nodded at both women, but the terrified look on his face betrayed his youth and inexperience. Maria guessed Carlos to be about eighteen, unusually tall, and probably of European descent. She and Isabella had the more typical Mayan heritage of most migrants from Central America. She wondered if Carlos' family might be wealthy and able to pay a high ransom for his freedom.

It was still dark when the truck pulled up to the gate in front of a large, white stucco house. Their driver got out, unlocked the gate, and then drove the truck up to the front entrance which was covered by an ornate Greco-Roman style portico. Maria noticed other cars and trucks parked nearby; she wondered how many other migrants were being held here against their will and how many other kidnappers used this house as their base of operation. One of the kidnappers suddenly stepped into the bed of the truck and pushed her to the ground, jolting Maria back to the present. The three hostages were quickly led into the house through an impressive set of heavy wooden double doors. Every move they made seemed to echo in the huge entry hall where they paused before being shoved into another large, nearly empty room to their left. There, a man brought water for the hostages and allowed them a brief respite. Their next stop was a visit to one of the bathrooms on the first floor. After quickly relieving themselves, they were led down a hallway to much smaller rooms in the back of the house.

Maria and Isabella were pushed into a windowless room with two small cots, and Carlos was shoved into the next room. Before leaving them, the kidnapper demanded their cell phones. Maria was thankful that Jorge had their family's only phone. At least her kidnappers would not be able to contact any family members, saving all except Jorge from great fear for her life. Isabella relinquished her phone; the kidnapper stuffed it in his jacket pocket and locked the doors to their rooms, departing without another word.

It was nearly morning but Maria and Isabella were exhausted from their night-long ordeal. They both fell asleep immediately and had no sense of what time had passed when two men unlocked their door and burst into their room, reeking of alcohol and marijuana. One man stumbled to Isabella's bed while the other went to Maria. She recognized him as the kidnapper from their truck ride with the long scar on his face. Maria held up her arms but he held her down.

He leaned down within inches of Maria's face and growled, "Give me your husband's phone number now." Maria didn't say a word. She knew that Jorge didn't have enough money for her ransom, and she did not want these evil men to threaten him or Sofia. She bit her lip as her attacker began pulling down her pants.

The other man held Isabella's arms in a vise-like grip as she struggled and screamed. In a drunken voice, Isabella's attacker announced, "We have your family's phone number, thanks to your cell info. But now you'll watch while your friend pays with her body for not giving us what we want."

While the assault was over very quickly, it felt like an eternity to Maria. She turned her face to the wall but the foul breath of her attacker made her feel sick. In her anguished thoughts, she prayed: *Please God, make it end. Please, God.* When her attacker rolled off the bed and pulled his pants up, he turned back to Maria and said, "I will do this every day until you give us your husband's phone number." Maria was motionless until the two men left their room; it was then that she turned over and threw up all over the floor next to her cot.

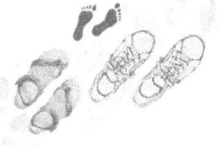

CHAPTER 12

SO CLOSE

It seemed so unfair that he was less than a mile from the U.S border and yet Maria was - well - who knows where she was.

As the two police officers drove Jorge to the Reynosa hospital, Jorge told them about the gang attack on the bus and how his wife and two other migrants were taken hostage. He was struck by how unperturbed the officers were. They asked him a few questions about his wife's appearance and status of her pregnancy, but they wrote nothing down. When Jorge challenged how seriously the officers would investigate his report, their reply was discouraging.

"We will make a report. But you have to understand that there are hundreds of kidnappings each year in the state of Tamaulipas. Our resources are stretched very thin. We are sure that you will get a call from your wife's kidnappers, demanding a ransom. We suggest that you pay the ransom because we will be unlikely to find her. These gangs are very smart."

The officers let Jorge out at the Emergency Room

entrance to the hospital. The modern, large hospital ER was crowded with people waiting to be seen, outside sitting on benches, and standing in lines leading inside. Many of the people in line appeared to be migrants with children. Some looked sick while others looked merely exhausted. Jorge felt fortunate that his gunshot wound allowed him to get in for treatment ahead of the others, even though the officers left him there with no offer of assistance after he was discharged. The Emergency Room doctor, a harried-looking man with a slight American accent, reassured Jorge that the wound was superficial; he bandaged it quickly after removing the bullet. His arm in a sling, Jorge was back on the street outside the hospital within a few hours. After getting directions from other migrants still in line outside the hospital, Jorge began walking back to the shelter.

It was late afternoon and the streets of Reynosa were bustling with all kinds of people. Jorge walked along a city sidewalk that bordered a small park. A Mariachi band played just inside the wooden fence, its lively tunes drifting through the air far beyond the city park. At least ten men in traditional Mexican costumes played trumpets, Spanish guitar, *vihuela*,[6] and *guitarron*.[7] Families were standing around the band, some singing and clapping to the music. Many of the onlookers appeared to be migrants from Central America, all here in Reynosa, waiting for their chance to realize the American dream.

The festival-like atmosphere in the park contrasted with the anxiety Jorge felt, especially when he saw women clutching small children. He was overwhelmed with the rage

---

6   A high-pitched five string guitar
7   A small-scaled acoustic bass

he felt toward his wife's kidnappers. It seemed so unfair that he was less than a mile from the U.S. border and yet Maria was – well – who knows where she was. He wanted to kill the man he saw pushing his wife out of the bus. They were supposed to be here together, resting and making plans for how to get across the Rio Grande River. Instead, he is here in Reynosa, alone with Sofia, unsure of anything anymore. Jorge quickened his pace, eager to reach the shelter where Sofia would be waiting for him.

He rounded a corner and stopped short at what he saw just ahead. Two men were beating a third man on the sidewalk, hitting him in the stomach. The man fell to the sidewalk and the two attackers started kicking him. After a brief moment in which Jorge sized up the danger, he quickly crossed the street to avoid the fight. He felt a pang of guilt at not helping the man being attacked, but he knew that he wouldn't be much help with his arm in a sling. Jorge wasn't the only one to dodge the attackers. Not only were people fleeing rather than helping; no one seemed to be calling the police on their phones. Jorge surmised that violence in Reynosa could well be as rampant as what he had left behind in his hometown in Honduras.

Jorge walked a block out of his way to make sure he wasn't the next victim of a mugging. He sat down on a sidewalk bench and put his head in his hands. Suddenly, Jorge felt ill. His head was swimming and sweat broke out all over his body. *I think I'm having a nervous breakdown,* Jorge thought as he sat alone on the bench in this violent city. In the last 24 hours, Jorge was shot; watched his wife being kidnapped; went to a huge hospital in a new city; left his daughter in a shelter; and witnessed a mugging. Despite his fragile state of mind, Jorge again allowed his thoughts to settle on Maria. He had no doubt that she was being held for ransom and he wondered why he had not received a call demanding payment. For about the twentieth time since he had arrived in Reynosa, Jorge pulled his phone out of his pocket and checked for voice messages. Nothing. Was it possible that Maria refused to give his phone number to her kidnappers? Perhaps she was no longer able to give it to them. The possibility of his wife being hurt or killed was too much for Jorge and he quickly banished the thought. The only thing that mattered at this moment was his daughter.

Jorge took a deep breath and tried to calm himself down. One more slow breath in...slow breath out and he felt himself reconnecting to his present reality. He got up from the bench and continued walking in the direction of the Catholic shelter. He hoped that Sofia was finally getting some sleep after she had calmed down somewhat from the trauma of her mother being taken away from her.

As he approached the shelter, the sight of the children playing in the yard alleviated some of Jorge's anxiety. The Catholic Church had been a source of comfort and assistance throughout Jorge's life. When he was a child, members of his parish helped his family by building a working sewage system in his home. Funds were provided by the Church for Jorge to continue his education past the ninth grade. Neither Jorge nor his sisters resented attending mass several times a week. On the contrary, they enjoyed the sense of spiritual celebration and community they felt in the presence of the local priest and others who believed as they did.

It seemed fitting to Jorge that, once again, he was relying on the Church to help him and his family. He went inside the shelter and found Sister Edna setting the table for dinner. She greeted him warmly and asked him about his shoulder injury.

"I am very lucky that my wound was superficial, Sister," Jorge replied.

"I'm sure you're wondering how your little girl is doing," Sister Edna commented. "Sofia went to bed after a big lunch and she is still sleeping comfortably. Come with me and we'll go to see her." Sister Edna led Jorge to the back of the shelter where there were several rooms with bunk beds.

"This is the room for women and children and here is Sofia," Sister pointed to Sofia with a smile. "Your room is across the hall, where all the men sleep. Pick out one of the available beds. I need to get back to my dinner chores, but we can talk later about your needs."

Jorge was brought to tears by the sight of his daughter sleeping so peacefully. This scene brought back memories of a happier time when Sofia was a toddler – before their desperate family trek became a necessity. He said a quick prayer for guidance and even gratitude, despite his present difficulties.

He turned to Sister Edna and whispered, "Sister, I can't thank you enough for your help. I don't know what I would have done if you had not welcomed Sofia and me into this shelter. And yes, I want to talk with you about my wife, Maria, and hear what you think I should do."

"That is my job, Jorge, and I praise God for this opportunity to help you and so many others like you," Sister Edna said. "God loves you. Never forget that," she added. "Now, get some rest and then clean up for dinner. We eat at 7 pm. Don't be late."

"Daddy, you're back!" Sofia cried with joy when she woke up to see her father standing over her.

Jorge and Sofia embraced and Jorge felt as if his heart would burst. He gave a quick prayer of thanks to God for keeping him alive to take care of his beautiful little girl. No matter what lay ahead, he vowed that he would somehow get her across the border safely and provide her with a life that he knew would make Maria happy.

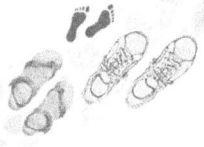

CHAPTER 13

SO FAR

The only thing that loomed ahead, as Maria saw it, was a choice between rape and betrayal.

Isabella jumped from her bed and rushed over to Maria. She climbed into Maria's bed, cradled her, and cooed, "It's alright now. He's gone."

After a few minutes, Maria whispered, "I've never been with anyone except my husband. I feel so...dirty."

Isabella didn't reply. Stroking Maria's hair, she finally uttered "You are very brave, Maria."

Despite Maria's determination to be strong, she couldn't stop her tears. She was grateful for Isabella's compassion, but she longed for her husband to hold and comfort her. Above all, she longed for Jorge to rescue them. As Maria saw it, the only thing that loomed ahead was a choice between rape and betrayal. She wondered if she should surrender to the kidnappers' demands and give them Jorge's cell number. She quickly played out the consequences in her mind. If the kidnappers called her husband, he would probably lie and promise payment. Then what? How would he get the money? Maria thought that the bus had probably arrived in Reynosa by now and Jorge was in the process of getting medical treatment. She wondered if he told the police about the kidnapping. Maria had heard too many stories about widespread corruption on the Mexican police force to think they would be of any help. For all she knew, they may be in partnership with the gang that kidnapped her.

After a sleepless night, someone unlocked their door and shouted for Maria and Isabella to use the bathroom. After cleaning up her vomit from the previous night, Maria headed for the bathroom. As she used the toilet, Maria noticed some blood in her urine. *Oh no,* she thought. *Not this. I can't lose my baby.* Maria called out for Isabella, who came running.

"What's wrong, Maria?" Isabella asked, voice pitched high with anxiety.

"I'm bleeding. Just a little though," Maria said, trying to sound calm.

Isabella had never been pregnant but she had witnessed miscarriages among women in the migrant caravan. She knew that the trauma and stress that Maria had endured could very well trigger a miscarriage.

"Should I tell anyone?" she asked Maria.

"No, definitely not," Maria responded. She regretted telling Isabella what happened. But the fear of losing her baby made her react without thinking.

"Hopefully, the bleeding will stop and everything will be fine." Maria tried to calm herself once again.

While the two women were in the bathroom, someone banged on the door and said, "Hurry up. There are clean clothes in your room. We're coming to get you in five minutes."

After dressing, Maria and Isabella were taken to the kitchen. There they were told to cook and clean for the rest of the day. The two women quickly realized that this house was more than a stash house. It was a working farm that fronted the cartel's various businesses. The sun had barely risen when at least twenty men came into the house looking for breakfast. Maria caught sight of Carlos among the men. He nodded but there was no opportunity to talk privately. As he drew closer, Maria noted his soiled clothing, dirty neck and even dirtier hands. He had been put to work in the fields. He looked tired already, and Maria wondered if Carlos had ever done any manual labor. Some of the men looked like Mexican farmers to Maria, while others reminded her of the gangs that roamed the streets of her hometown. The man with the long scar on his face was among them; he snickered at Maria when she set a platter of eggs on their table.

"Did you sleep well, Mommy?" he laughed. Maria didn't respond. She felt bile surge into her throat.

The kitchen was well-stocked, with more food than Maria had ever seen in one home. There were two refrigerators and a large, professional stove. The pantry was filled with bags of dried beans and jars of salsas. Maria counted at least five frozen chickens and dozens of packages of beef in the freezer. *This is quite a large operation,* she thought. *I wonder who oversees all of it?*

As if to answer Maria's question, a man sauntered into the house and looked around. All the other men froze and looked at him expectantly. Without a word, the man walked behind the long kitchen counter where Maria and Isabella were working. He slowly, menacingly looked both women up and down, resting his gaze briefly on Maria's belly.

"Your husband must not care about you or your unborn child since you are here." The apparent boss commented loudly to Maria.

The man with the long scar broke in before Maria could speak. "She doesn't have a phone and she refuses to give us her husband's number. It won't be long though, before she changes her mind," he continued. The other men laughed loudly.

Maria didn't respond to the boss. Her humiliation at the comment from her rapist was only equal to her anger. *How dare this pig of a man speak of me this way!* she thought. *I will stab him if he tries to rape me tonight.*

With that thought, the kernel of a plan began to form in Maria's mind. The boss sat down at a table with the other men and Maria turned to Isabella.

"Get a knife and hide it under your clothes. I will do the same," she whispered.

The two women spent the entire day cooking and washing clothes. No sooner had Maria and Isabella cleaned up from one meal, it was time to start the next one for all the men on the farm. By 8:00 PM, Maria could barely stand up. After they were escorted back to their room, both women hid their knives under their pillows.

"Isabella," Maria said. "Let's see what happens tonight. If the rapists come to our room again, we may have an opportunity to stab them. The room is dark and they won't see us. When I say the word 'pig,' we attack. Can you do this, Isabella?"

"I am not sure, Maria. These men are strong. If we aren't

successful, they will kill us." Isabella countered. "If we are successful, then what do we do? The noise will attract the others. If we make it out of the house, where do we go? You can't run in your condition."

Maria admitted that Isabella's concerns were valid. She hadn't thought through the dangers well enough. She sighed deeply. She just couldn't bear the thought of being raped again and doing nothing to defend herself. She felt helpless and so far away from Jorge or anything familiar. Should she give her kidnapper Jorge's cell number? What difference would that make? She expected to be murdered no matter how she and Isabella resisted. Just as Maria's thoughts were spiraling downward, she caught herself.

Jorge won't let us be murdered, Maria thought. *He will do anything to get us out of this place. He may be on his way with help right now. We need to be patient. I know he will rescue us soon. God is on his side and on our side.* She turned over and closed her eyes.

That instant, the man with the long facial scar and his companion from the previous night burst through the door. "Both of you...take off your clothes," the man ordered gruffly.

CHAPTER 14

COMPASSION

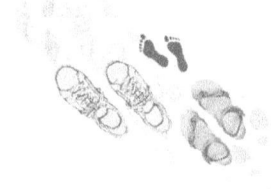

Most of them had little or no money but after listening to Jorge's plight, many offered to help him with donations toward a potential ransom payment. Twenty pesos here; fifty pesos there.

Jorge found that he was the center of attention at dinner that evening in the shelter. Other migrants were eager to hear about the kidnapping and what had happened to Jorge's shoulder. No one was surprised that his bus had been attacked. Many of the others had witnessed kidnappings themselves or heard stories from others. Jorge was touched by the outpouring of empathy and support he received once he shared his personal experience. Without exception, every resident in the shelter had experienced loss in their home communities – loss from murder, violence, and poverty. However, the idea of a husband losing his pregnant wife to kidnapping and then continuing on the journey north with his small child seemed like the height of suffering to everyone who heard Jorge's story. Most of them had little or no money but after listening to Jorge's plight, many offered to help him with donations toward a potential ransom payment. Twenty pesos here, fifty pesos there. Jorge was overwhelmed at the kindness extended by his fellow migrants.

After dinner, Sofia was invited to play outside with several mothers and their children. Now free to speak seriously without upsetting his daughter, Jorge sat down with Sister Edna and a few other migrants to discuss Maria's unthinkable situation and possible interventions. As director of the shelter, Sister Edna was acutely aware of all aspects of the migrant crisis in Reynosa. One of the other migrants in the group was a witness to a famous kidnapping in which nineteen male migrants were abducted from a bus by a gang working for one of the rival Gulf drug cartels. He speculated that Maria's kidnappers might be from the same gang, especially if the two attacks occurred close to one another.

Since Jorge's bus was stopped in the middle of the night, he was unable to ascertain exactly where his wife's kidnapping took place. However, he did remember a few landmarks on the highway, including a distinctive billboard that displayed American President Donald Trump as a monster with the slogan *Make America Great Again* printed on a U.S. flag in the background. The billboard was infamous in Mexico; the migrant who offered clues as to the possible gang involved in Maria's kidnapping knew exactly where it was located. It was a billboard of great prominence on the same highway where the earlier kidnapping had occurred.

Sister Edna was aware of the growing use of kidnapping as a money-making tactic of the drug cartels. The notorious incident in which the nineteen migrants were kidnapped caused great concern to everyone associated with the migrant community. Sister Edna was familiar with that area of Tamaulipas and knew where local cartel houses were rumored to operate. In particular, she had heard about a large working farm that was widely believed to front a Gulf cartel operation. One of the released hostages from the earlier kidnapping told a police officer that he was forced to work on a vegetable farm that concealed poppy fields. He was too frightened to say much, since his family had paid a ransom for his release. However, the officer revealed to Sister Edna that the released hostage described migrant women working in the kitchen on this farm. It was apparent that these women had been kidnapped along with many of the field workers.

As Jorge listened, his interest and excitement grew. Could Maria and the two other kidnapped migrants be on this farm? The more he heard about the previous kidnapping, the more determined he was to travel to the farm to see if Maria was there. Of course, he knew how dangerous this would be. He would need help.

"Sister Edna, should we call the police?" Jorge asked.

"The Mexican police are known to be deeply corrupt, Jorge," Sister Edna replied. "They have done nothing to shut down this cartel, despite the fact that they've known about this farm for a while. They will not help you and if you inform them of your plan, they may tip off the cartel. Maria will be in even greater danger if that happens."

"I can't just leave her there!" Jorge cried with desperation. He would rather die trying to rescue Maria than abandon her to the cartel.

"Jorge, you have to think about Sofia," Sister Edna urged him. "What would it be like for her if she lost both parents? I beg of you to think about paying a ransom. It is really your only option. I pray you will receive that telephone call in the next day or so. Try to think positively. I've heard that the gangs will often accept low ransoms for their hostages. Ever since the government started cracking down on cartels and more arrests have occurred, gangs are looking for different ways to make money. They know that migrants don't have much money, so you can offer a low amount and they may return Maria to you. I'm going to bed now and I think you should, too. You've had a very long and difficult day."

With that, Sister Edna left the room and Jorge turned to the other migrant. "If I don't hear from Maria's kidnappers tomorrow, will you help me find someone who will drive me to the cartel farm?" Jorge asked.

"Yes, of course," came the immediate reply from Jorge's new friend. "I think I know someone who may be able to help us."

At that moment, Sophia came in from her play and Jorge walked with her back to the room designated for women and children. It was after 9 pm and many of the shelter residents were already asleep. After Jorge got Sofia ready for bed, he tucked her into her bunk and listened as his daughter recited her nightly prayers.

"God, thank you for giving us this nice place to rest.
Thank you for Sister Edna who makes us good food.
Thank you for Mommy and Daddy.
God, I miss Mommy so much.
Pleases make the bad men bring her back to me and Daddy.
If Mommy comes back,
I promise to be good and never ask for anything again."

Jorge had to turn his head so that Sofia wouldn't see his tears. "I love you, Sofia. Sleep well and I'll see you in the morning," he whispered.

Jorge found an empty bunk bed in the men's dormitory and climbed in. As he lay there listening to the snoring and groans among the other men, he thought about everything that had happened to him, Maria, and Sofia since they left their home and began their long and dangerous trek. Heat, exhaustion, abuse, hunger, pain, fear, kidnapping - yes, they had experienced real suffering. But Jorge also thought about the many people who extended kindness and compassion to him and his family. He thought of the smiling villagers in Guatemala who clapped and offered encouragement to the hundreds of migrants who walked together through their country. He remembered the kind priest at the Arriaga shelter who welcomed them after their harrowing trip on The Beast. And now he and Sofia were comforted by the compassion of Sister Edna and the other migrants here in Reynosa. Jorge realized once again how blessed he was to have his beautiful daughter in his life. He gave a prayer of thanks to God, closed his eyes, and was asleep in minutes.

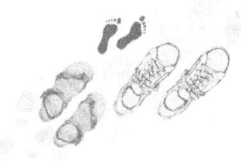

CHAPTER 15

BROKEN

One of these nights when I am raped, I'll fight back with my knife. They will kill me then, and I will be spared further suffering.

It was hard to imagine how Maria's assaults by her kidnapper could get any worse. But they did. She and Isabella took off their clothes, as the men demanded. Then, the man with the long facial scar started laughing. "You're getting really fat, Mommy," he said as he pointed a flashlight at Maria in the darkness. "But don't worry. You will still enjoy what I'm going to do to you. But first, Mommy, give me your husband's cell phone number."

When Maria didn't reply, her attacker looked at Isabella and then turned back to Maria. "Okay, now your friend will have to pay for your unwillingness to do what you are told," he said ferociously to Maria.

While his companion held Isabella down, he pulled out a knife, walked over to Isabella and slashed her right cheek. Maria screamed as blood began to trickle down Isabella's face. The attack happened so quickly that Isabella didn't respond initially. Then, when the sharp pain registered, she let out a high-pitched wail.

"Now your friend looks like me and no man will marry her. It is all your fault, Mommy," the attacker snarled at Maria. "One more chance. What is the phone number?" When Maria still didn't comply, the man pulled out a scarf and handed it to his companion, who was still restraining Isabella.

"Tie this around her mouth before you *do* her. That way, you won't have to see the blood," he said to the other attacker.

Maria felt like she was in a nightmare that had no end. While the man with the scar raped her, she slowly slid her hand behind her head and under her pillow. She felt the knife. *Now is my chance,* Maria thought. Should she stab her rapist? A split second later, she made her decision. She pulled her hand back and screamed, "I'll give you my husband's phone number. Just stop hurting us!"

Maria's attacker stood up and smiled. He put on his pants and pulled out his cell phone from the pocket. The other man did likewise, leaving Isabella lying on the bed with a blood-soaked scarf tied around her mouth. Both men typed Jorge's phone number into their phones.

"You've made the right decision, Mommy," Maria's attacker said with an air of satisfaction. "You might be back with your husband by tomorrow. Of course, maybe he won't want you anymore. Get some sleep. You have to make us breakfast in a few hours."

As soon as the men left, Maria ran over to Isabella and untied the scarf. Pressing the scarf on Isabella's cheek to stop the flow of blood, Maria whispered, "I'm so sorry, Isabella. It is all my fault. I should have given him Jorge's phone number right away. Then, maybe he wouldn't have cut you. When he was raping me, I wanted to stab him right then – but I realized you were right. We didn't have a chance fighting back against them. If I had tried to stab him, he would have killed both of us. I am so sorry that he cut you."

Isabella squeezed Maria's hand and said, "Please don't blame yourself. Since I don't have any family members who could pay a ransom, I know it is only a matter of time before they kill me. One of these nights when I am raped, I'll fight back with my knife. They will kill me then, and I will be spared further suffering. But with you it is different. I know God will keep you safe and return you to your family."

The two women held each other quietly, weeping over their difficult lives, their gutted dreams, and their growing realization that fate would likely separate them forever.

A few hours later, Maria and Isabella were roused to begin another long day of cooking for the farm workers. In the brief time they were given to dress and bathe, Maria washed and bandaged Isabella's lacerated face. The only thing she could find in the bathroom cabinet were *Band-Aids* and Maria joked that Isabella looked like a walking commercial for the bandage company.

Breakfast that morning consisted of *chilaquiles*,[8] scrambled eggs, and fruit. As Maria carried the plates to the farm workers seated around the four square tables in the large kitchen, she again noticed Carlos, who met her glance with dejected, tired eyes. He didn't dare say anything, especially since the crew's boss sat at his table.

Despite the fact that Carlos's bedroom was next to the

---

8 Fried corn tortillas popular in Mexico

room shared by Maria and Isabella, there was no opportunity to communicate. Maria speculated with some level of humiliation that Carlos probably heard the sounds coming from her room at night. She tried not to think about what she and Isabella endured at the hands of these cruel kidnappers. It was too horrific.

Shifting to other thoughts, she also wondered about the issue of ransoms. *Carlos' family is probably wealthy and will pay a high ransom,* Maria reflected. *But Jorge won't have much money to pay for me. Maybe Isabella and I will both die here. I'll never see my beautiful Sofia again.*

Despite her determination to keep tight control over her emotions, these thoughts were more than Maria could bear. Her hands began shaking uncontrollably; a full plate she was carrying crashed to the floor close to the boss. *Oh no! How could I be so careless?* Maria thought to herself. She bent over awkwardly, clutching her large belly as she tried to clean up the spilled food.

"Niña estúpida!" the boss jumped up and shouted at Maria. "Clean that up and get out of my sight!"

Hearing the commotion, Isabella came out from the kitchen and helped Maria clean up the mess. At the sight of Isabella's face covered with Band-Aids, the men started laughing. "Look at her. Her face is the funniest thing I've ever seen!" One man laughed derisively as he pointed at Isabella.

Somehow, Maria and Isabella made it through the morning, only to be rewarded by the taunts all over again during *comida.*[9] Maria noticed that her attacker and his boss were missing from the group. Then, just as most of the farm workers began eating their first course, a rich vegetable soup,

---

9 The main meal of the day in Mexico

both men walked into the room.

The man with the long facial scar approached Maria and whispered. "When the meal is done, you are going to Reynosa, Mommy. I told you that you made the right decision by giving us your husband's phone number. So I guess you will miss me. Right?"

Maria couldn't believe what she was hearing. She didn't respond immediately but Isabella did. She grabbed Maria and hugged her close.

"I knew you would be seeing Jorge and Sofia soon. I am so happy for you," Isabella said joyfully.

As the news sank in, Maria couldn't stop smiling. At the same time, she felt guilty at the prospect that she would be leaving Isabella behind. She looked at Isabella and said through tears, "Jorge and I will figure out a way to get you out of here, Isabella. I promise."

"Don't worry about me, Maria," Isabella replied softly. "God will take care of me."

After Maria and Isabella finished washing the dishes from the comida, they were surprised to see one of the kidnappers bringing Carlos into the kitchen. For the first time since their ordeal began, Carlos was smiling; Maria quickly realized that he was also being released. She and Carlos were blindfolded and led outside to the vehicle that would return them to their loved ones.

I'm free! Thank you, God! Maria thought to herself. She could hear Isabella's sobs growing fainter as Maria left her friend behind.

CHAPTER 16

CADEJO

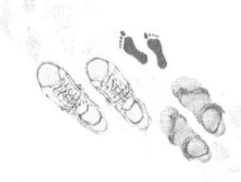

---

*"My Mommy and Daddy are going to get me a dog when
we move into our new house in the U.S.," Sofia said to the
woman. "He will be big and grey and I will name him
Cadejo."*

Everyone who utilized the services of the shelter was
expected to help with cooking, cleaning, yard maintenance,
and child supervision. The 120-bed facility was almost full;
residents were coming and going every day. The activity
would seem chaotic to a visitor, but Sister Edna ran a tight
ship, made certain that everyone knew the rules, and posted
a weekly schedule for easy reference. It was late morning.
Jorge and another migrant were helping Sister Edna with
some heavy lifting at the shelter. Bunk beds needed to be
moved in the men's dormitory twice each week so that the
task of mopping could be completed.

This shelter, run by the Catholic Daughters of Charity,
had been in operation for over fifteen years. It was staffed
by four nuns, one of whom was Sister Edna – director for
the last eight years. Volunteers from the local diocese also
helped with many of the shelter's programs. When the

shelter opened, most of the residents were migrants who were trying to reach the U.S. border and needed respite while they waited for asylum. While the current residents were also migrants, most of them were no longer trying to reach the U.S. They had already tried to cross the border and failed. The shelter's residents were primarily migrants who were deported from the U.S. back to their home countries.

The shelter received over 1,000 deportees a month. Three weekly airplane flights from across the U.S. first brought the deportees to the border. There, they took a bus to the migrant shelter. If they had already made arrangements with their families, a shelter stay was not necessary. Those who did stay were typically migrants originally from Central America who were deported without any money, resources, or the means to communicate with their families. Most remained at the shelter for about three days, though they could stay longer if they had special health or legal needs. Some of the deportees were eager to get back to their families; they worked in Reynosa just long enough to cover the expense of a bus ticket home. Others who didn't have family usually ended up working longer in Reynosa.

Earlier in the morning, Jorge had gently awakened Sofia. After quickly washing their faces and brushing their teeth, they joined the other residents in the meeting room for a Morning Mass. Following Mass came breakfast, which today consisted of *Machacado con Huevo*.[10] Jorge and Sofia were not familiar with the dish, but Sofia couldn't seem to eat her meal fast enough.

She looked at her father and said with a smile, "This is

---

10   A dish popular in Northern Mexico consisting of shredded dry beef, scrambled with eggs

good, Daddy. Can we have this for breakfast every day?"

Jorge smiled wistfully, thinking how much Sofia reminded him of Maria. Her smile, her big eyes, her zest for life – all made Jorge desperately miss his wife and wish she was there with them as a family. *I wonder what Maria is doing right now,* he thought, trying not to let his fear overtake him. "If you like it, we'll have it every morning, *mijita,*"[11] Jorge replied as he softly stroked Sofia's hair.

Sofia continued eating her breakfast while Jorge's thoughts drifted to his childhood days in Honduras, when he first met Maria. He thought she was the prettiest girl he had ever seen. He met her at school, where she was a year behind him. She was shy and studious and he was smitten immediately. When he finally asked her for a date, she didn't reply at first. He thought maybe she didn't like him. But after a few moments, she looked at him with that sweet smile. "If my father approves, then yes, I will go out on a date with you."

Maria's father had approved and Jorge took Maria to an afternoon movie, followed by ice cream in the park. He had saved his money for a long time for this opportunity to impress Maria. From that moment on, he knew they were meant for each other. Maria was sweet, but sassy and smart. She was innocent but adventurous. They looked out for each other and had hopes for the future. He loved her more than anything else in the world. Now, Jorge looked at Sofia and felt a rush of love that was every bit as strong as what he felt for his wife.

"Daddy, is Mommy coming back today?" Sofia asked the question as if there was an easy answer. "I hope she does so that I can show her the drawings I made. Did you like

---

11 My little daughter

my pictures, Daddy? I like it here. Will we stay here after Mommy comes back?"

Sofia was jumping up and down as though her feet were on springs. Jorge reached for her and hugged her to him. "You ask a lot of questions, *mi chica tonta!*"[12] Jorge replied. "Now, go play on the swings with the other children."

Sofia ran out the back door to the fenced backyard. The yard had a swing set and a large play set that included a sliding board and two-story climbing tower. Several children were kicking around a soccer ball, but Sofia headed straight for the sandbox. She eyed the efforts of two other girls who were trying to build a house out of sand. One of the migrant women was sitting in the grass next to the sandbox. "Come join us, *princesa!*" the woman welcomed Sofia to the pair playing in the sandbox.

"My Mommy and Daddy are going to get me a dog when we move into our new house in the U.S.," Sofia said to the woman. "He will be big and grey and I will name him *Cadejo.*[13] Cadejo will make sure the bad men never hurt us again."

The woman didn't reply to Sofia but she thought that she should share the little girl's comment with her parents, or maybe with Sister Edna. In any case, the woman understood Sofia's fears. Most of the migrants in this shelter had been through hell on their journeys north. *We could all use an animal spirit to keep us safe,* the woman thought to herself.

Jorge made sure his daughter had supervision in the backyard before he headed to the men's dormitory to help move furniture. He joined two other men who had signed

---

12 My silly girl
13 A mythical animal spirit in Honduras which looks after children

up for the chore of mopping the floor. The room wasn't very large but eight sets of bunk beds were crammed, end to end, against the walls. Every bunk bed set had duffel bags and backpacks stuffed underneath. After the men moved everything to the middle of the room, they mopped around the walls.

Just as the men were about to move the bunk beds back into place, Jorge's cell phone buzzed in his pocket. His heart leapt into his throat when he saw the name of the caller. "Hello? Yes, I can pay for my wife. I don't have much money but I will give you all I have – $500.00," Jorge said into the phone with a trembling voice. There was a pause and Jorge responded, "Yes, I understand. I will be there at 1:00 pm."

With that, Jorge sank to his knees and shouted out to everyone in the dormitory room. "My wife is being freed! The kidnappers accepted my ransom offer!" Everyone cheered and Jorge whispered a prayer of thanks to God for bringing Maria back to him. He ran out into the backyard to share the good news with Sofia.

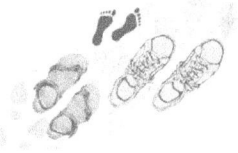

CHAPTER 17

THE SECRET

Their relationship had always been based on honesty, but Maria worried that no good would come from telling him.

Maria and Carlos sat in the back seat of the pick-up truck, blind-folded and hands tied. It was an uncomfortable two-hour drive to Reynosa. The back seat was not really designed for passengers and Maria was especially cramped, her legs pulled up to her belly. Neither of them said a word during the trip, although Maria tried to pick up any information she could from the conversation going on in the front seat. She heard the two men discussing where they would meet Jorge – La Carnada Grill, a well-known restaurant on Boulevard Jose Maria Morelos, in downtown Reynosa. Apparently, the men planned to park several blocks away and leave Carlos in the truck with one man while the other walked with Maria to the restaurant. After the exchange, the men planned to drive to a small town nearby to release Carlos to his family.

As the truck neared the restaurant, Maria thought about her reunion with Jorge and Sofia. She tried to suppress her excitement in case something went wrong, but every time she pictured herself seeing Jorge her heart skipped a beat. She also had plenty of time in the truck to ponder a serious dilemma – should she tell Jorge about her rape? Their relationship had always been based on honesty, but Maria worried that no good would come from telling him. His pain and anger over Maria's rape would only add to the suffering they had both endured on this trip. She told herself she just wanted to forget about the rape and get on with her life – a life she hoped would only get better after she, Jorge, and Sofia crossed the border.

Maria knew, however, that she would never be able to forget what happened to Isabella and her in the farmhouse. The thought of her rapist's foul breath and dirty hands made her shudder. Maria wondered if she would ever feel clean again. She had scrubbed herself raw when she showered each morning, but she couldn't wash away the memory. Would she be able to make love with her husband without that memory intruding?

How can I keep this secret from Jorge? Maria wondered, as she tried to get in a more comfortable position in the back seat of the truck. *He will suspect something is wrong every time he touches me, and he will blame himself.* Maria reflected on the many times Jorge stood by her on the family trek north. She thought about Jorge's fight with the kidnappers on the bus. She remembered how he protected her and Sofia on the rooftop of The Beast. She even remembered how he tenderly bandaged her blistered feet in Arriaga. Maria resolved right then and there not only to tell Jorge the truth, but to do so knowing that he would hold her blameless.

However, she found it more difficult to forgive herself.

She wondered if she could have done more to thwart her kidnapper's assaults. Maybe she should have stabbed the man with the long facial scar when she had the chance. When she and Isabella were making breakfast at the farmhouse, could they have escaped out of the back door while the men were eating? As she second-guessed herself, her thoughts went to Sofia. All of her decisions during her kidnapping ordeal were made knowing that she must stay alive for Sofia's sake – and for her unborn baby. Maria touched her belly and felt her baby kick.

Maria also thought about Isabella. *I have to tell Jorge what they did to Isabella. When I tell him that Isabella was raped and cut, he will immediately wonder if I was attacked, too. This is another reason I have to tell him the truth.*

Maria leaned over to Carlos, trying not to arouse suspicion. She whispered, "Carlos, I wish you luck and may God bless you."

Carlos replied in a serene voice, "I am so happy to be out of that place. God blessed us both. I'll never forget you, Maria."

His words helped Maria relax. *Carlos seems so calm and happy,* Maria thought. *He knows that God saved us from our nightmare. I need to stop being so hard on myself. I did the best I could for myself, for Jorge, and for Sofia. Jorge and I have always been honest with each other, and I'm not going to stop being honest now. I'll tell Jorge everything that happened and that I did what I thought was right. I need to trust Jorge and I need to trust myself.*

Maria smiled and felt the strong bond with Carlos – a bond that could only exist between people who have been through hell together. She wondered what kind of life Carlos was returning to and how much ransom his family paid for his return. She also couldn't help but wonder how large her own ransom was and how Jorge was able to raise any money at all.

As they had planned, the kidnappers parked the truck two blocks away from the restaurant. One kidnapper hastily jumped out and pulled his seat forward to enable Maria to get out. He untied Maria's blindfold and hand ties. When Maria had difficulty getting out of the truck, the kidnapper grabbed her by the hair and pulled her out violently, causing her to fall. Maria stifled her cry of pain. As he pulled her up roughly, the kidnapper said into her ear, "You stupid bitch. I'm glad to be rid of you. Just remember that if you say anything to the police about us, we will find you and kill you and your entire family. Now, walk with me to the restaurant as if we are friends. I have a gun so don't try to run."

Despite the terrifying outset, the remainder of Maria's exchange for ransom proceeded without a hitch. She was instructed to walk casually up to Jorge in order not to attract attention. However, Jorge received no such instructions. He raced down the sidewalk in front of the restaurant to Maria and hugged her fiercely, releasing her only long enough to hand an envelope full of cash to her kidnapper. The kidnapper turned abruptly without a word and walked away from the couple. The encounter outside the restaurant lasted less than three minutes, but Maria's joy was enough to last her a lifetime.

Maria and Jorge spent the next hour inside La Carnada Grill, holding hands across the table and catching up on what had happened to each of them. Despite her resolve, Maria couldn't stop her tears of shame as she shared what she and Isabella had endured at the hands of their kidnappers. When

Maria finally found the courage to look into Jorge's eyes; all she saw was love. She needn't have worried about Jorge's reaction to her assault; he had anticipated her story. He knew what monsters these men could be, and his anger quickly evolved from a desire for vengeance to a desire to help Maria heal from her experience.

When Maria paused from telling her story, Jorge said softly, "Maria, all that matters is that we are together again. What happened was not your fault. I will love you forever." He held her hand tightly and waited for her to calm down.

Finally, Maria said, "Jorge, I promised Isabella we would help her get out of there. What can we do?"

"I think we should talk with Sister Edna and some of the other shelter residents to figure out what we can do without making it worse for Isabella." Jorge replied. "I met a man who has connections in the police department. He can be trusted. But for now, I know a little girl who can't wait to see her mama!"

When Sofia got her first glimpse of her parents getting off the bus at the street corner adjacent to the shelter, she ran to the front gate, screaming "Mama, Mama!" The joyous reunion was shared by everyone at the shelter, including Sister Edna, who rushed toward Maria almost as quickly as Sofia. Everyone was eager to hug Maria and share in the Hernandez family's reunion.

As they all went inside, Sofia clung to her mother's shirt hem. She looked up at Jorge and said, "Daddy, we won't let any bad men take Mommy ever again, will we?" Jorge felt a lump in his throat as he picked up his daughter and carried her into the shelter. He whispered into Sofia's ear, "No, we won't let any bad men take Mommy ever again."

CHAPTER 18

WELCOME TO THE U.S.

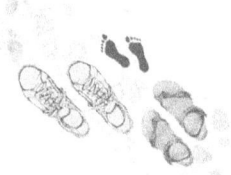

As the agent led Jorge to the bus that would take him and hundreds of other husbands and fathers to their separate detention facility, Sofia cried out, "Daddy, don't leave us!"

The first step for all migrants seeking asylum in the U.S. is to have a "credible fear" interview with an asylum officer from U.S. Customs and Border Protection (CBP). Credible fear is an asylum law concept in which the migrant must convince the CBP officer that his or her fear of returning home is credible. Fear can be based on five categories: race, religion, nationality, political opinion, or membership in a particular social group. Economic factors such as fleeing poverty are not typically admissible. Under international law, the U.S. may not return a person to a country where they may face torture or other serious harm. These obligations toward asylum-seekers originate in the UN Convention Relating to the Status of Refugees, also known as the 1951 Refugee Convention.

Once an asylum-seeker "surrenders" himself to a border agent at a port of entry, the individual receives a case number. This number indicates how many people are ahead of him in the process. Because the number of asylum-seekers has increased so dramatically in the *last few years, there is a months-long backlog of migrants waiting to have their credible-fear interview at the southern border.*

As a family with a very young child and another on the way, it is likely that Jorge, Maria, and Sofia would be placed in a U.S. family detention center until their credible fear interview could be held. The wait could be for many months. There was a strong possibility that the family would be split up during their wait and a likelihood that, despite all the difficulties the family had endured to get to the point of seeking asylum, in the end their application would be denied. Without evidence of real harm awaiting them back in Honduras, they would probably be deported – either to Mexico or back to Honduras.

Luckily, the kidnappers released Isabella early the next morning. From conversations with Sister Edna and other migrants, Jorge learned that Carlos' father – wealthy and well-connected with both legal and dubious affiliates - quickly paid Isabella's ransom once Carlos was safely delivered to his family. Maria was elated to hear that her friend had been released. She vowed to locate Isabella once she, Jorge, and Sofia finally settled in the U.S.

Sister Edna extended the Hernandez family's shelter stay another week so that Maria could rest and see a doctor. During that time, Jorge and Maria also sought advice from volunteer attorneys regarding the best way to seek asylum in the U.S. Much of the discussion centered on what was best for Sofia and for Maria's unborn child.

Jorge and Maria were made aware of several options for seeking asylum. If they attempted to cross the Rio Grande River, they could try to evade border authorities and blend into the crowds of McAllen, Texas. Sister Edna and the volunteers discouraged the couple from seriously considering this option for several reasons: it would brand them illegal;

the river was dangerous and would likely prove too diffi-cult for Sofia and Maria; successfully evading border agents would be nearly impossible; and finally, it was widely known that criminal gangs smuggled many migrants across the Rio Grande. Jorge and Maria wanted to avoid any further contact with gang members at all costs. If the family surrendered to border agents at the McAllen Port of Entry, they could seek legal asylum, a lengthy and difficult process. A final option for the Hernandez family was to remain in Reynosa, delaying their dream of crossing the border.

Most of the deportees Jorge met at the shelter planned to find jobs and housing in Reynosa, at least temporarily. While jobs were available, crime in Reynosa was as bad as it was at home in Honduras. Migrants were easy targets for gangs. Jorge heard stories of daily robberies at bank teller machines and violent assaults on neighborhood streets. Women were frequently kidnapped for ransom, and crimes associated with buying and selling drugs were rampant. As if all of these circumstances weren't enough to make Jorge and Maria reticent about life in Reynosa, they were also aware that the Mexican authorities warned tourists to avoid visit-ing Reynosa and the entire surrounding state of Tamaulipas. They simply couldn't seriously consider staying in Reynosa any longer than what was necessary. Though extremely grateful to Sister Edna for all her support while they were at the shelter, both Jorge and Maria agreed that life there beyond the protection of the shelter would be too dangerous.

Jorge and Maria were shocked to hear the stories of bru-tal conditions at U.S. family detention centers. No one had told them they might be separated from Sofia or from each other. Sister Edna was careful not to influence their plans, but she knew that the current U.S. government administration did not welcome these immigrants. On the contrary, it demonstrated disdain for Central Americans fleeing toward safety – a notable departure from past administrations. Sister Edna's religious convictions and her job required her to do everything she could to protect the desperate migrants from further suffering. Unfortunately, she knew there were no perfect answers. She prayed every day for change in immigration policy on both sides of the border. Even more fervently, Sister Edna prayed for compassion toward migrants in all the situations they routinely faced.

Despite their fears of being separated by U.S. authorities, Jorge and Maria believed the only choice they had was to surrender at the border. What drove their final decision was not the goal of saving their own lives, finding better jobs, or avoiding rape and assault. What they valued most and what drove them to undertake this journey was the goal of providing their children with a much safer future than the one available to them if they had stayed in Honduras. There was no question in either Jorge's or Maria's mind that if they went back to Honduras or Mexico, their children would not survive. After weeks on their dangerous trip north, the family found themselves in line with hundreds of others like themselves at the Customs and Border Protection (CBP) border port of entry at McAllen, Texas.

Once inside the large fenced CBP office building, the migrants were given an application for seeking asylum. The application was lengthy and confusing, and many migrants weren't able to navigate it effectively. Fortunately, Jorge's ability to read and write English enabled him to progress through the application successfully. The advice Jorge had received from the volunteer attorneys at the Reynosa shelter helped him answer the questions thoroughly, avoiding the "trigger words" that would immediately disqualify the family's request for asylum. Sofia was frightened by the crowds and the noise inside the building, but Maria kept her close, reading stories to her daughter from a stack of paperback books given to them by Sister Edna. When Maria introduced her curious little daughter to *El Gato Ensombrerado*,[14] Sofia managed a bright smile and quiet laughter. Reading this story and its sequel to Sofia was the perfect way to keep her calm and entertained while Jorge completed the onerous paperwork.

After completing the application for asylum, the family waited for the next step in the process. Two hours later, a caseworker briskly greeted Jorge and Maria and handed them each a card that indicated their family case number – 19,523. This meant that the family's wait time until their scheduled credible fear interview would be months – not weeks. Because Maria was seven months pregnant, she and Sofia would be held at the family detention center in Dilley, Texas. Jorge would be transported to a separate detention facility for men, about 50 miles from Dilley.

Maria was stunned by this news. She would likely give birth in the detention center, without Jorge at her side. "How could the president allow us to be separated when I give birth?" she cried to the agent.

"I understand your concern, Mrs. Hernandez," the agent replied curtly. "We don't have the resources to house men in Dilley and we certainly don't have the resources to transport one man fifty miles to Dilley on short notice, which would

---

14 *The Cat in the Hat*

be the case in a birth situation."

Jorge knew better than to show his anger to the agent. Instead, he tried to reassure his wife. "We will figure this out, Maria. Don't worry. At least you and Sofia will be safe and you will get medical care when the baby comes. The time will go by quickly and we will be together soon."

As the agent led Jorge to the bus that would take him and hundreds of other husbands and fathers to their separate detention facility, Sofia cried out, "Daddy, don't leave us!" Maria drew her close and thought to herself, *How could this happen? Why would the U.S. government do this to us? We are not criminals. We are honest people wanting a better life for ourselves and our children. How could this be?*

Maria had been warned not to expect comfortable accommodations at the Dilley Center, but their first night in detention was more like a nightmare than merely an uncomfortable stay. Upon arrival, agents led Maria, Sofia, and the thirty other migrant women and children from their bus to the *hielara*[15] – where they would try to sleep on the concrete floor or benches. A Mylar sheet that seemed a lot more like aluminum foil than a blanket was their only cover. Bathroom breaks were infrequent; both women and children soiled themselves, horrified at the lack of privacy they were afforded and the loss of dignity they were experiencing. No accommodations were made for Maria's pregnancy; she was concerned that many of the women and children had bad colds. The sounds of crying mixed with coughing, sniffling, and sneezing continued throughout the night. By the next morning, many of the women gave in, completely exhausted by the torturous conditions in the hielara. They lined up to

---

15   The ice box; a frigid building with concrete floors

request deportation. Maria couldn't help but wonder if that was the intent of the experience.

*Give us your tired, your poor...*a phrase Maria had often comforted herself with over so many miles of difficult travel. She had always heard about Lady Liberty welcoming migrants from all countries to the U.S. Now, she wondered if their current circumstances were just a way of weeding out the strong migrants from the weaker ones. Maria was determined; she was strong and resolute. She and Sofia would survive this challenge as they had so many others on their way here.

After their first night in the hielara, the new residents were taken to the *perrera.*[16] *At least it's warmer here,* thought Maria as she and Sofia joined three other mothers and their children in a "kennel." They spent three days and nights in the perrera with no books or toys for the children and little opportunity to get exercise. No one was allowed to shower. Meals consisted only of bologna or ham sandwiches and water. The only entertainment was a TV installed high on the wall. These unhealthy conditions led to more requests by detainees for deportation. By the time Maria and Sofia left the perrera, they had both caught colds and Maria's feet and ankles were alarmingly swollen. She had not received any medical attention since her arrival almost a week earlier.

The South Texas Family Residential Center is the largest immigrant detention center in the United States. Opened in December 2014 in Dilley, Texas, it is owned and operated by CoreCivic, previously known as "Corrections Corporation of America." The Center has a capacity of 2,400 and is intended to detain mainly women and children from Central America. When Maria and Sofia arrived, the center

16 Doghouse; chain link cages similar to dog kennels

was at full capacity.

CoreCivic is a profit-making company that contributed $250,000 to the U.S. President's inauguration in 2017. The company had a $1 billion contract with the U.S. Department of Homeland Security to operate several facilities designed to either incarcerate or detain various populations. As the center in Dilley filled up, CoreCivic had difficulty providing adequate staff and resources to meet the needs of families. Numerous complaints from advocacy organizations about inadequate medical and specialty services led to changes in policy regarding family detention. Despite the company's recent decision to curtail lengthy family detention due to limited resources, increasing numbers of women arriving with small children and infants made it difficult to release them quickly without a social service network of support.

Maria and Sofia were finally assigned to one of the many tiny family cottages at the facility. Although generously described as "cottages" in company literature, they were very sparse wooden structures, laid out in rows, not unlike the infamous Japanese internment camps of World War II. Maria and Sofia shared their cottage with one other family. Each cottage had one bedroom, one bathroom, and one kitchen. The detainees were not allowed to use the kitchen, ostensibly due to safety concerns. While the detainees could freely walk anywhere on the grounds of the center, its entire perimeter was fenced with chain link which was topped with barbed wire. Detainees were not allowed to leave the center; in effect, the detention center was a prison.

In stark contrast to their first few nights at the center, Maria and Sofia adapted to the less restrictive environment they found after moving into the cottage. Twice, Maria was taken to San Antonio for an obstetric evaluation. She was also able to meet with a volunteer attorney who arranged for her to speak weekly to Jorge by phone. Sofia began attending onsite classes which were taught by state-licensed teachers. In keeping with her friendly personality, Sofia quickly made friends with other children, especially in the computer lab.

In her 38th week of pregnancy, Maria went into labor. Although Jorge was not present for the birth at a San Antonio hospital, he was able to speak with Maria shortly after she delivered a healthy baby boy. In their delight, they again discussed several possible names. After a few minutes, Jorge and Maria agreed upon their earlier choice. Their new son's name would be Miguel.

The family had been in the custody of the U.S. government for six weeks and their new case number was 2,204.

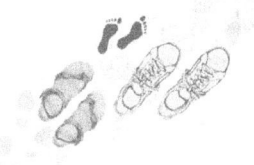

Chapter 19

Detention

Few of these desperate migrants from Central America realized what they would face when they applied for asylum in the United States.

Jorge's experience at the Karnes Family Residential Center was very different from Maria's and Sofia's in the South Texas Family Residential Center in Dilley. While many families remained undisturbed while in the Karnes Center, hundreds of other immigrant men and their sons were separated under the government's "zero-tolerance" immigration policy before finally being reunited by order of a federal judge. Protesting the separations and generally poor conditions at the center, many of the families at the Karnes facility mounted a hunger strike, with parents refusing to eat or drink and children declining to participate in scheduled school activities. At one point some of the men were hand-cuffed, re-separated from their children, and taken to the South Texas Detention Complex in Pearsall, Texas, more than 90 minutes away. The men were returned to the Karnes Center within days, but the incident was widely viewed as "payback" for the migrants' protests.

Jorge did not participate in the protests; however, he witnessed aggressive enforcement behaviors by center officers, including frequent use of offensive language and heavy reliance on force. These prison-like tactics only reinforced resentment and resistance by the migrants. Jorge was shocked at what he saw at the Karnes Center and he wondered if the stories of American respect for human rights were simply myths. He couldn't wait to be reunited with Maria and Sofia and he diligently monitored the progress of their asylum claim.

Immigrants in immigration court do not have a right to government-appointed counsel. However, legal advice was available to the detained migrants at the Karnes Center through RAICES, a nonprofit immigrant legal services group. Founded in 1986 as the Refugee Aid Project by community activists in South Texas, RAICES has grown to be the largest immigration legal services provider in Texas.

Recently, RAICES filed a legal suit against ICE, accusing them of creating barriers for people held at the Karnes, Texas detention facility to meet with legal teams. Barriers that were cited included:

· Barring RAICES volunteers from the visitation center for legal meetings until there was one prospective client or current client for every volunteer legal team member in the room.

· Reducing the number of detainees that RAICES volunteers could meet with daily.

· Terminating the practice of allowing people to sign up for legal help through a "walk-in" sign-up list.

Madeline Garza, a pro bono attorney with Raices, met with Jorge once while he was detained at the Karnes Center. "Jorge, I understand that your wife just gave birth to a baby boy. Congratulations! I'm just sorry that you've been separated from her and your children," Madeline said.

"Yes, it's very hard. We've never been apart before for this length of time," Jorge replied.

"I'm also sorry that you signed the document that gives ICE consent to deport you and your family." Madeline said. "The whole system is set up so people don't have lawyers. The first thing they do is try to get you to sign away your rights."

Jorge reacted with alarm. "I thought I did everything the lawyer at the shelter in Reynosa told me to do," he cried.

Madeline took a deep breath and said, "I have to be honest with you. It is likely that ICE will deny your claim for asylum, Jorge. Only about 15% of applications for asylum are approved. However, we can appeal that rejection and you will have your opportunity to fight it in front of an immigration judge. That could take a year or longer. ICE will release you and your family into the community as long as you promise to attend your scheduled court date. However, here is the worst part. You cannot get a legal work permit until your application is approved."

Jorge was indignant. "How can this happen? Why didn't someone tell us? No one in Honduras or on our journey north ever said these things. We have endured so much just to be turned away."

Madeline had heard this kind of reaction a hundred times before. Few of these migrants from Central America realized what they would face when they applied for asylum in the United States. Most of them would be deported immediately. If they got a lawyer to fight for their case, they would have a much better chance of their application getting approved. Severe restriction on each migrant's ability to get a work permit was a deliberate effort to further encourage their voluntary deportation. She didn't tell Jorge that a new government proposal would make it even more difficult for migrants to get a work permit.

"There are some ways you can apply for a work permit if ICE doesn't review your case within 180 days. But I strongly advise you to get a lawyer to represent you in that process," Madeline replied to Jorge.

Jorge slumped in his chair and said quietly, "I used all our money to get here. Then I had to raise money to pay a ransom for Maria's release from the drug gangs in Mexico. How am I supposed to pay for a lawyer?"

Madeline leaned forward and spoke earnestly, "Jorge, I know this is bad news, but there are many organizations and many people who care about you, your family, and the other migrants who want a better life in the U.S. Yes, it is a long, difficult process, but RAICES and other legal aid organizations will help you."

Jorge thought about all the times the Catholic Church had helped his family back in Honduras, and then again in Mexico. He wondered if the Church would help him again here in the U.S.

Madeline gave Jorge some information on how to prepare for the credible fear interview and then said, "I want you and Maria to study these questions and practice your answers. Okay? Then, no matter what the outcome, I want you to call me after you get a decision on your application for asylum. We'll figure out everything that happens next. Please don't give up." Madeline gave Jorge her business card and smiled, "Don't lose this!"

Ten days later, Jorge met his new son for the first time when he boarded the bus that took his entire family to their credible fear interview at the ICE office in San Antonio. As he started down the aisle, he heard Sofia cry out, "Daddy!" She raced toward Jorge and threw herself into her father's arms. "Daddy, I have a new baby brother! His name is Miguel and he's so cute! Come see!" Jorge grabbed Sofia's hand and they both made their way to where Maria sat, cradling the three-week old infant her arms. Tears were streaming down Maria's face as she handed Miguel to Jorge.

The migrants on the bus erupted into cheers as Jorge held his son for the first time. He looked at Miguel's perfect little fingers and his beautiful dark eyes and he said, "This is the happiest day in my life!" To Maria, Jorge mouthed the words, "*te quiero.*"[17]

A migrant across the aisle from Maria kindly gave his seat to Jorge so that the happy father could sit near his family. Jorge handed the baby back to Maria and sat down, Sofia climbing into his lap and chattering wildly about all her new friends at the South Texas Family Residential Center. Jorge couldn't stop smiling as he glanced at Maria and his new baby boy.

"No matter what happens in San Antonio, Jorge," Maria said, "We will always have each other. Everything will be alright."

Jorge's anxiety about the upcoming credible fear interview was far away, at least for that moment.

---

17 I love you.

CHAPTER 20

WHAT'S NEXT?

"Where are Itzel and her baby?" Maria asked.

Maria was nervous as she walked into the USCIS office with Jorge, Sofia, and Baby Miguel. Miguel had been fussy on the bus, and the noise and commotion of the hot waiting area hadn't helped. Their credible fear interview was scheduled for 11 am, but by the time they were finally called into the small interview office, it was after 1:00. Maria, concerned at the delay, knew that it wouldn't be long before Sofia's exhaustion and hunger would result in whining. She wondered, too, about nursing a hungry baby during the interview. *I want to do everything just as they expect I should to give us the best chance possible for things to go well, but Miguel will be inconsolable if I don't nurse him.* She pondered what her best move would be.

Jorge and Maria practiced their answers several times before going into the interview. However, they noticed that a number of other families in the waiting area had attorneys with them. Jorge and Maria couldn't afford a private attorney and Madeline Garza was not available. Jorge brought all the paperwork he had to support their request for asylum, but he knew that without a valid visa, their application might be denied. *Surely,* Jorge thought, *these government officers know that we can't go back to Honduras. They must know that our lives are truly in danger and that we are telling the truth.*

The asylum officer who conducted their interview was polite but not very friendly. Jorge and Maria were prepared for all her questions and were starting to feel more confident until Miguel started crying. Maria walked around the room, attempting to soothe the baby, while Jorge tried to concentrate on the interview. It wasn't long, though, before Sofia started tugging on Jorge's sleeve and whining, "Can we go now, Daddy? I'm hungry."

Sweat began to form on Jorge's brow but he gave Sofia a hug and said in her ear, "Shhh! Just a little while longer, Sofia. Then we'll eat."

The interview took almost an hour, after which the officer informed Jorge and Maria they would receive a decision within approximately 10 days. In the meantime, they would continue to be detained separately – Jorge in Karnes City and Maria and the children back at the South Texas Family Residential Center in Dilley. After eating and getting back on the bus, Jorge and Maria reflected on their views of the credible fear interview. They were hot, exhausted, and uncertain what their future might hold.

"I don't think we will be granted asylum, Maria. We didn't have a visa and the only other evidence we could offer was newspaper clippings – the one about Miguel's murder in Honduras and the other about your kidnapping in Mexico.

The officer seemed interested in your comments about the kidnapper's warning – that you shouldn't reveal any details to anyone or they would kill all of us. What do you think they'll decide about our application?"

"I am more confident than you are, Jorge. I think it was in our favor that the officer was a woman. She understands that our children will not be safe in either Honduras or Mexico," Maria replied as she started to nurse Miguel. "God will take care of us," she added.

When their bus arrived at the ICE Detention Center in Dilley, Sofia was visibly distraught as she said goodbye to her father. She clung to Jorge as Maria gathered up the baby and his diaper bag and began to walk up the aisle.

"I don't want you to leave us again, Daddy!" Sofia wailed.

Jorge tried to comfort his daughter, but his eyes teared up and his voice trembled as he replied, "Sofia, it won't be so long this time. I need you to be good and help your Mommy take care of Miguel. Will you do that?"

Sofia nodded and turned reluctantly to follow her mother. When she got to the bus door, she turned for one last look at Jorge, yelling, "I love you, Daddy." Once outside the bus, Maria and Sofia waved as it left for Karnes City. A guard checked their ICE identification papers and let them inside the chain link fence gate in front of the main building.

As they walked around the building on the path leading to the "cottages," Maria noticed only a few detainees outside. *This steamy Texas summer day probably drove most of the mothers and their children inside,* Maria thought. When they reached the cottage they had left at 5 am that morning, Maria opened the door to find a doctor and an ICE officer inside. The other family that currently shared their cottage was nowhere in sight.

"Hello, Mrs. Hernandez," the officer greeted her. He was not smiling "This is Dr. Ruiz. He would like to do an examination of Miguel."

"Why?" Maria demanded, her voice shrill with immediate anxiety.

"Now don't worry, Mrs. Hernandez," the officer replied, smiling unnaturally. "This is just a precaution. The flu seems to be spreading among the children here and we are required to examine all the children under two years of age."

Maria knew that many of the children at the center had been sick for the last week. Last night, Daniella, the 6-month old daughter of Maria's housemate, Itzel Ramirez, had cried and coughed throughout the night. When Maria and her children left early that morning, Itzel said Daniella was running a high fever.

"Where are Itzel and her baby?" Maria asked.

Dr. Ruiz responded slowly, "Mrs. Ramirez didn't tell us until this morning that Daniella was so sick. Unfortunately, there was nothing we could do to save her. The baby passed away this afternoon."

Maria now knew why there were so few detainees outside. They were either in the clinic, having their children examined or they were quarantined inside their cottages. Maria handed over Miguel to the doctor and sat down on a chair. The news of Daniella's death knocked the breath out of her.

How could this happen in the U.S.? she thought, but did not dare say aloud. *There are so many children in this center, and no one seemed concerned about them, at least not until now,* Maria mused.

Dr. Ruiz gave Miguel a thorough examination and

handed him back to Maria. "Your baby is not running a fever and doesn't have any congestion," he said. "That is good news, isn't it? Please let us know if any of you start to have any symptoms, okay?"

Maria nodded and replied. "Yes. Thank you." All she could think about was poor Itzel and how traumatic it would be if she lost Miguel so unexpectedly.

The ICE officer turned toward Maria and spoke as he moved toward the cottage door. "I'm sending a housekeeping aide over here tonight to give this cottage a thorough cleaning. She should be here around 7 pm."

The flu epidemic among the children in the detention center made national news, but fortunately Daniella was the only detainee to succumb. Maria noticed that a nurse now visited each cottage twice a week to check on every family member's health. Maria and the other mothers kept their children inside most of the time and when they were together, they talked about how things in the U.S. weren't as wonderful as they had been led to believe. Despite the problems, however, most of the families believed they had made the right decision in leaving their homes and countries. They wanted their children to lead safer, better lives; nothing would deter them from this goal.

Exactly ten days later, Jorge and Maria each received identical letters from the USCIS informing them that they were found to have a credible fear of returning to their home country. They would be afforded the opportunity to apply for asylum "defensively," which meant, according to Madeline, they could request asylum in immigration court. At that time, an immigration judge would decide whether or not the family would be granted asylum. The Hernandez family was not granted access to the less complicated "affirmative asylum process" because they did not have visas. While the defensive asylum process requires significant wait time until the court date, it does imply that the asylum officer believed the applicant had a significant possibility of being eligible for asylum.

Maria and Jorge were overjoyed that they were not denied asylum. Maria's immediate response when Madeline explained the letter to her on the phone was "Prayer works!"

Jorge was less enthusiastic but still hopeful. He asked with some weariness, "What's next, Madeline? Where do we go? How do we support our family?"

As Madeline predicted, Maria and Jorge were not eligible to apply for work permits while they waited for their court dates. This could take months, if not years, and there are no government programs to provide for a waiting family's needs. However, Madeline knew of many church-based programs in California that provided housing and services for immigrants like the Hernandez family. She found a housing program in the agricultural region of California; a vacant church had been repurposed to provide reasonably comfortable living for 8–10 families with children.

As for work, Madeline carefully explained that Jorge and Maria should avail themselves of whatever opportunities they could find with the help of their non-profit service provider. She also strongly advised them to stay in touch with her. It was imperative that she or another attorney from RAICES accompany them to their scheduled immigration court date. "If you don't show up for your court date," Madeline warned the couple, "You will be deported immediately. The government has the authority to keep your children here in the US while they deport you to Honduras. Since Miguel was born here, he is a US citizen. The government would definitely keep him here and put him into a foster home. Sofia might be deported with you but there's no guarantee. So don't miss your court date!"

After detaining them for so long, it seemed to Jorge and Maria now that ICE couldn't wait to release them. Madeline made sure that ICE lived up to its obligations to provide the Hernandez family with a few changes of clothes and enough money to get to their destination in California. Within 48 hours after receipt of their letter of approval, the Hernandez family was on a bus again.

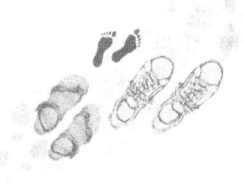

EPILOGUE

FIELD OF DREAMS

"Was it worth it?" Maria quietly asked her husband.

LIFE FOR FARMWORKERS IN THE U.S.

- *Farmworkers are not protected under the National Labor Relations Laws.*
- *Farmworkers are exempt from many protections under the Fair Labor Standards Act (FSLA).*
  - *They are exempt from most minimum wage and hour guarantees.*
  - *They are not entitled to overtime pay or mandatory breaks for rest or meals.*
  - *There are few labor protections for farmworker children.*
  - *Farmworkers are not protected from retaliation by federal law when engaged in labor organizing.*
- *Women farmworkers are often systematically subjected to sexual slurs, groping, threats, beatings, and even rape in the fields.*

- *There are an estimated 10,000 to 20,000 cases of physician-diagnosed pesticide poisoning among U.S. farmworkers, and the average life expectancy of farmworkers is 49 years.*

  http://www.farmworkerfamily.org/information

The idealism that sustained the Hernandez family during their desperate trek from Honduras to the U.S. border continued when they headed eagerly to California. They had managed to endure unimaginable hardships along the way but believed that the worst was now behind them. They dreamed of what America promised – good jobs, a good education for their children, and living free from violence. California awaited them like a shining beacon.

However, nothing prepared them for the next three years of their lives in the heart of the American bread basket - the San Joaquin Valley in Central California. The Hernandez family was one of three families sponsored by a large, wealthy Protestant church near Fresno, California, where most of the members were executives or managers of the local corporate farms. In exchange for their free housing in the vacant church, Maria and Jorge were expected to join hundreds of other migrants working in the local almond and strawberry farms. Sofia attended a local public school and infant daycare for Miguel was provided at the sponsor church. In the beginning, Maria and Jorge were grateful for the assistance. It soon became clear to them, however, that this help came at a steep price.

Both Maria and Jorge routinely worked 10-12 hours a day, six days a week in the strawberry fields of the San Joaquin Valley during the growing season. Despite their long days, they only earned $9 an hour, well below the minimum wage in California. By the time they retrieved Sofia and Miguel in the evenings, they were too tired to do anything as a family other than share the evening meal. Maria, who had always been prone to migraine headaches, found it difficult to get through a day of physical labor outside without taking pain medication, especially with daily temperatures typically in the high 90s. Her increasing incidence of headaches affected her crop-picking production, resulting in poor work evaluations. Field supervisors were quick to reprimand any farmworker who seemed to lag behind the standard set for production. As time went on, Maria grew increasingly depressed over her working conditions, and this further exacerbated her headaches.

Like many other migrant farmworkers, Jorge suffered respiratory ailments continuously. Because there were no sick benefits for farmworkers, Jorge rarely took a day off, especially as Maria's health deteriorated. However, what bothered Jorge the most was the family's inability to save money. Despite their rent-free housing, they never seemed to have enough money for anything other than the basics. They were completely tied to the church for their survival, and they saw no prospects for anything better in their future. At one time, Jorge dreamed of buying a little house for his family and even starting his own business in auto repair. After three years, his dream seemed further away than ever.

Despite their disillusionment with their own lives, Sofia's quick adaptation to life in California gave her parents the motivation to carry on. She had a quick mind and a fun-loving personality, enabling her to do well in school and make friends easily. To her parents, it seemed that Sofia had become an American overnight. They loved listening to her stories about what she learned in school and her escapades with the other children. Within a year, Sofia was practically fluent in English, delighting her parents enough so they forgot their worries about the future. Maria and Jorge hoped for the same bright future for their toddling son, Miguel.

Three years later, the Hernandez family returned to Texas for their court appearance and USICE judgment on their application for asylum. This time, Madeline Garza, their RAICES attorney, accompanied them and helped present their case to the judge. The result? The immigration judge ruled in favor of the Hernandez family's application, enabling the family to apply for a green card.

As Maria, Jorge, Sofia, and Miguel headed back to the bus that would take them back to their lives in the fields of California, Jorge and Maria stopped simultaneously and looked at each other.

"Was it worth it?" Maria quietly asked her husband.

Jorge looked at his happy children and then back at Maria. Only in her thirties, Maria's face was lined and covered with brown spots from the sun. Jorge's hands were calloused and he coughed every few minutes. He smiled briefly and replied with a tinge of sorrow, "We can't go back."

References

Prologue: The Terror Begins

Hume, M. (2014, November 14). *Why the murder rate in Honduras is twice as high as anywhere else.* Retrieved from http://theconversation.com/why-the-murder-rate-in-honduras-is-twice-as-high-as-anywhere-else-34687.

McVicar, J. (November 07, 2018). *Why are so many people fleeing Honduras?* Retrieved from https://www.americamagazine.org/politics-society/2018/11/07/why-are-so-many-people-fleeing-honduras.

Why is Honduras so violent? Impunity, gangs, drugs, poverty, and corruption. Retrieved from https://www.ajs-us.org/content/why-honduras-so-violent?gclid=CjwKCAjw1dzkBRBWEiwARO-VDLBKtrQQOshYUIXPOukSwdRbsHRKBuEi-ORlF5FtwF-Gy4hNCgKypl8hoCqVAQAvD_BwE.

Wikipedia. (2019, June 18). *Crime in Honduras.* Retrieved from https://en.wikipedia.org/wiki/Crime_in_Honduras.

Chapter 1: Leaving Home

Arthur, A. (2019, March 25). Stop ignoring the crisis at the border. Retrieved from https://cis.org/Arthur/Stop-Ignoring-Crisis-Border.

Buschschlüter, V. (2019, March 12). *Migrant caravan: I pray to my dead daughter, says mother from Honduras.* Retrieved from https://www.bbc.com/news/world-latin-america-47474316?intlink_from_url=https://www.bbc.com/news/topics/cq23pdgvg7xt/honduras&link_location=live-reporting-story.

Silman A. and McVeigh, S. (2018, December 12). *When you can't go forward and you can't go back.* Retrieved from (https://www.thecut.com/2018/12/talking-to-the-women-of-the-migrant-caravan.html.

Chapter 2: Mexico

Bonello, D. (2018, November 6). *100 people kidnapped from migrant caravan by drug cartels in Mexico.* Retrieved from https://www.telegraph.co.uk/news/2018/11/06/100-people-kidnapped-migrant-caravan-drug-cartels-mexico/.

Bonello, D. and Siegal, E. (2014, September 14). *Is rape the price to pay for migrant women chasing the American dream?* Retrieved from https://splinternews.com/is-rape-the-price-to-pay-for-migrant-women-chasing-the-1793842446.

Driver, A. (2018, November 13). *An intimate look at life inside the migrant caravan.* Retrieved from http://time.com/longform/migrant-caravan-mexico/.

Fieury, A. (2016, May 4). *Fleeing to Mexico for safety: The perilous journey for migrant women.* Retrieved from https://unu.edu/publications/articles/fleeing-to-mexico-for-safety-the-perilous-journey-for-migrant-women.html.

Schrank, D. (2019, June 5). *Mexico meets migrants at southern border with armed forces.* Retrieved fromhttps://www.reuters.com/article/us-usa-immigration-trump-mexico/mexico-meets-migrants-at-southern-border-with-armed-forces-idUSKCN1T62YC.

Chapter 3: The Beast

Arthur, A. (2019, March 25). Stop ignoring the crisis at the border. Retrievedfromhttps://cis.org/Arthur/Stop-Ignoring-Crisis-Border.

Cortes, J. (2019, April 26). *Hundreds of migrants in southern Mexico board The Beast heading north.* Retrieved from https://news.yahoo.com/hundreds-migrants-southern-mexico-board-beast-heading-north-185038819.html;_ylt=AwrE19.cXApdGEcAkChXNyoA;_ylu=X3oDMTEyZnBzbDVmBGNvbG8DYmYxBHBvcwMxBHZ0aWQDQjY4MzNfMQRzZWMDc3I-.

Stevenson, M. & Perez, D. (2019, April 24). *In Mexico, migrants turn to 'The Beast' after highway raids.* Retrieved from https://www.apnews.com/f46fd14d73484369ad441aa390953e01.

Tuckman, J. (2014, august 26). *Mexico plans boost to the Beast to discourage Central American migrants.* Retrieved from https://www.google.com/search?q=central+american+migrants+riding+The+Beast&-source=lnms&tbm=isch&sa=X&ved=0ahUKEwiHp8fy46LhAh-WNZd8KHb60Bm0Q_AUIDygC&biw=1229&bih=603#imgdii=rka H6jcP-2DkwM:&imgrc=9AewMR2Ueu0iTM.

Chapter 4: Sheltered

Cortes, J. (2019, April 20). *Welcome for migrants cools in Mexican town weary of caravans.* Retrieved from https://news.yahoo.com/welcome-migrants-cools-mexican-town-weary-caravans150857259.html;_ylt=AwrEze0UrQddo_oAwVxXNyoA;_ylu=X3oDMTEyO-GFjbzJnBGNvbG8DYmYxBHBvcwM5BHZ0aWWQDQjY4MzN-fMQRzZWMDc3I-.

Lazo, A. (2019, June 17). *Mexican shelters strained by migrants struggle with U.S. returnees.* Retrieved from https://www.wsj.com/articles/mexican-shelters-strained-by-migrants-struggle-with-u-s-returnees-11560763802.

Wardarski, J. (2014, September 25). *Along the route north, shelter operators heed calling to aid migrants.* Retrieved from http://cronkite-newsonline.com/2014/07/along-the-route-north-shelter-operators-heed-calling-to-aid-desperate-migrants/index.html.

Chapter 5: Hope

Agren, D. (2013, January 9). *Mexican priests work in shelters, helps shift migrants, evangelicals' perceptions.* Retrieved from https://www.catholicnews.com/services/englishnews/2019/pope-makes-donation-to-help-migrants-traveling-through-mexico.cfm.

Schmidt, D. (2019, February 5) *In search of the promised land: Hope and despair in the migrant caravan.* Retrieved from https://brooklynrail. org/2019/02/field-notes/In-Search-of-the-Promised-Land-Hope-and-Despair-in-the-Migrant-Caravan.

Chapter 6: The Road

Asmann, P. (2018, August 27). *Suspension of entire local police force shows depth of Mexico corruption.* Retrieved from https:// www.insightcrime.org/news/brief/suspension-entire-local-po-lice-force-shows-depth-mexico-corruption/...

Associated Press. (2018, October 28). *Migrant caravan to rest following report of abducted child.* Retrieved from https:// www.nbcnews.com/news/us-news/migrant-caravan-rest-following-report-abducted-child-n925331.

Bonello, D. (2019, June 10). *Why Lopez Obrador's vow to decriminalize drugs won't help Mexico.* Retrieved from https://www.ozy.com/opin-ion/why-lpez-obradors-vow-to-decriminalize-drugs-wont-help-mexico/94779.

Burbank, J. (2018, August 15). *Mexican cartels prey on migrants from Central America.* Retrieved from https://themobmuseum.org/blog/mexican-cartels-prey-migrants-central-america/.

Linthicum, K. (2019, March 13). *Mexico launching search for mi-grants pulled off bus by gunmen near the U.S. border.* Retrieved from https://www.latimes.com/world/la-fg-mexico-missing-migrants-20190313-story.html.

Chapter 7: Kindness

BBC.com (2018, November 7). *In pictures: Migrant caravan rests in Mexico City.* Retrieved from https://www.bbc.com/news/world-latin-america-46124651.

Perez, S. Stevenson, M, & Verza, M. (2018, November 18). *Migrants straggle into Mexico City to shelter at stadium.* Retrieved from http://www.chroniclet.com/national-news/2018/11/06/Migrants-straggle-into-Mexico-City-to-shelter-at-stadium.html.

VOA News.(2018, November 6). *Aid arrives for migrants at Mexico City stadium as US votes.* Retrieved from https://www.voanews.com/americas/aid-arrives-migrants-mexico-city-stadium-us-votes.

Chapter 8: Decisions

Associated Press. (2018, November 6). *Migrant caravan enters Mexico City to shelter at stadium.* Retrieved from https://wgntv.com/2018/11/06/migrant-caravan-enters-mexico-city-to-shelter-at-stadium/.

France-Presse, A. (2018, October 31). *Pregnant migrants want their children 'to be American'.* Retrieved from https://www.voanews.com/a/pregnant-migrants-want-their-children-to-be-american/4636956.html.

Malkin, E. (2018, November 10). *Mexico gave the migrant caravan a warm welcome. It wasn't always this way.* Retrieved from https://www.nytimes.com/2018/11/10/world/americas/migrant-caravan-mexico-city.html.

Reuters. (2019, January 31). *Migrants' caravan leaves Mexico City, bound for northern border.* Retrieved from https://mexiconewsdaily.com/news/migrants-caravan-leaves-mexico-city/.

Chapter 9. Kidnapped!

Arnada, T., Espinoza, J., & Del Angel, A. (2019, March 11). *Cartel gunmen kidnap 19 from passenger bus near Mexican border city.* Retrieved from https://www.breitbart.com/border/2019/03/11/cartel-gunmen-kidnap-19-from-passenger-bus-near-mexican-border-city/.

Smith. R. (2018, May 11). *Hundreds of people in Mexico are kidnapped every year. And the problem's getting worse.* Retrieved from https://www.vox.com/2018/5/11/17276638/mexico-kidnappings-crime-cartels-drug-trade.

Stargardter, G. and Gardner, S. (2014, October 14). *Migrants snared in multi-million dollar kidnap racket on U.S.-Mexico border.* Retrieved from https://www.reuters.com/article/us-usa-immigration-kidnapping-insight/migrants-snared-in-multi-million-dollar-kidnap-racket-on-u-s-mexico-border-idUSKCN0I10DJ20141013.

Chapter 10: Cartel

Davidson, J.D. (2019, April 4). *The Border crisis is a money-making machine for smugglers.* Retrieved from https://thefederalist.com/2019/04/04/border-crisis-money-making-machine-smugglers/.

Davis, K. (2016, October 21). *A Short history of Mexican drug cartels.* Retrieved from https://www.sandiegouniontribune.com/news/border-baja-california/sd-me-prop64-sidebar-20161017-story.html.

KGNS.TV. (2019, March 14). *Migrants kidnapped from charter bus in Mexico.* Retrieved from https://www.kgns.tv/content/news/Migrants-kidnapped-from-bus-in-Mexico-507148701.html.

González, D. and Solis, G. (n.d.). *A Human smuggler, and the wall that will make him rich.* Retrieved from https://www.usatoday.com/border-wall/story/human-smuggling-crossing-order-illegally-methods/559784001/.

Google.com images. (2019, June 19). *Cartel mansions in Mexico.* Retrieved from https://www.google.com/search?q=-cartel+mansions+in+mexico&source=lnms&tbm=isch&sa=X&ved=0ahUKEwjqgJTYo8jhAhXGVN8KHSy5BiEQ_UIDigB&biw=1229&bih=603#imgrc=aFmerKOFYp027M:.

Hennessey-Fiske, M. (2018, December 17). *On the Texas-Mexico border, no one knows who's smuggling the border crossers. Everyone's a suspect.* Retrieved from https://www.latimes.com/projects/la-na-roma-texas-immigration/.

Stewart, S. (2019, January 19). *Tracking Mexico's Cartels in 2019.* Retrieved from (https://worldview.stratfor.com/article/tracking-mexicos-cartels-2019.

Chapter 11: Assault

Fernandez, M. (2019, March 3). *'You have to pay with your body': The Hidden nightmare of sexual violence on the border.* Retrieved from https://www.nytimes.com/2019/03/03/us/border-rapes-migrant-women.html.

Kanno-Youngs, Z. and Averbuch, M. (2019, April 5). *Waiting for asylum in the United States, migrants live in fear in Mexico.* Retrieved from https://www.nytimes.com/2019/04/05/us/politics/asylum-united-states-migrants-mexico.html.

PBS.org (2014, March 31). *Women crossing the U.S. border face sexual assault with little protection.* Retrieved from https://www.pbs.org/newshour/nation/facing-risk-rape-migrant-women-prepare-birth-control.

Chapter 12: So Close

Miroff, N. (2019, February 5). *The Other reason the Mexican government is escorting migrants to the border.* Retrieved from https://www.washingtonpost.com/politics/2019/live-updates/trump-white-house/live-fact-checking-and-analysis-of-trumps-2019-state-of-the-union-address/the-other-reason-the-mexican-government-is-escorting-migrants-to-the-border/?utm_term=.84d3aa865618.

Miroff, N. (2019, March 15). 'The Conveyor Belt': U.S. officials say massive smuggling effort is speeding immigrants to — and across — the southern border. Retrieved from https://www.washingtonpost.com/national/the-conveyor-belt-us-officials-say-massive-smuggling-effort-is-speeding-immigrants-to--and-across--the-southern-border/2019/03/15/940bf860-4022-11e9-a0d3-1210e58a94cf_story.html?utm_term=.d2d01a8ae9a1.

Sieff, K. (2019, January 8). The U.S. sends thousands of deportees each month to Mexico's most dangerous border areas. Retrieved from https://www.washingtonpost.com/world/the_americas/the-us-sends-thousands-of-deportees-each-month-to-mexicos-most-dangerous-border-areas/2019/01/07/bbe4036e-ff45-11e8-a17e-162b712e8fc2_story.html?noredirect=on&utm_term=.e55c2f02ea93.

Chapter 13: So Far

Maldonado, D. (2017, August 11). US artist trolls Trump with billboard in Mexico City. Retrieved from https://www.google.com/search?q=billboards+in+Mexico&source=lnms&tbm=isch&sa=X&ved=0ahUKEwjFjIvprd3hAhWMl-AKHa30DHoQ_AUIDigB&biw=1229&bih=603#imgrc=ZFV_ullBAOCTTM:.

Smith, R. (2018, May 11). Hundreds of people in Mexico are kidnapped every year. And the problem's getting worse. Retrieved from https://www.vox.com/2018/5/11/17276638/mexico-kidnappings-crime-cartels-drug-trade.

Sang, L. (2019, February 20). Kidnappings, murders on the rise in Mexican state where woman was decapitated: 'There is a lot of suffering going on' Retrieved from https://www.foxnews.com/world/kidnappings-murders-on-the-rise-in-mexican-state-where-woman-was-decapitated-there-is-a-lot-of-suffering-going-on.

Chapter 14: Compassion

Ferguson, S. (2018, October 17). *Inside migrant shelters at the U.S-Mexico border*. Retrieved from https://www.unicefusa.org/stories/inside-migrant-shelters-us-mexico-border/34563.

Kahn, C. (2019, January 10). *In Mexico, Reynosa has become an unintended home for a growing number of migrants*. Retrieved from https://www.npr.org/2019/01/10/684145551/in-mexico-reynosa-has-become-an-unintended-home-for-a-growing-number-of-migrants.

Mashek, J. (2019, May 3). *What I learned helping migrants at the U.S.-Mexico border*. Retrieved from https://www.afsc.org/blogs/news-and-commentary/what-i-learned-helping-migrants-us-mexico-border.

Samuels. A. (2018, June 18). *Here's a list of organizations that are mobilizing to help immigrant children separated from their families*. Retrieved from https://www.texastribune.org/2018/06/18/heres-list-organizations-are-mobilizing-help-separated-immigrant-child/republish/.

Spagat, E., Merchant, N., & Espinoza, P. (2019, May 9). *For thousands of asylum seekers, all they can do is wait*. Retrieved from https://www.apnews.com/ed788f5b4269407381d79e588b6c1dc2.

Chapter 15: Broken

Flores. S. (2019, April 3). *We fled the gangs in Honduras. Then the U.S. government took my baby*. Retrieved from https://www.nytimes.com/2019/04/03/opinion/border-honduras-separation-gangs.html.

Hernandez, V. (2017, March 15). *Our world: Kidnapped in Mexico* Retrieved from https://www.huffpost.com/entry/our-world-kidnapped-in-mexico_b_9462258

Hastings, D. (2013, December 16). *Mexican cartels use social media to post gruesome victim photos, sexy selfies.* Retrieved from https://www.nydailynews.com/news/world/mexican-drug-cartel-thugs-post-atrocities-social-media-article-1.1515860.

Chapter 16: "Cadejo"

Chapin, A. (2018, November 1). *Children in the migrant caravan are getting faint, feverish and sick.* Retrieved from https://www.huffpost.com/entry/migrant-caravan-children-getting-sick_n_5bda65fee4b-0da7bfc16f83f.

Haag. M. (2019, February 27). *Thousands of immigrant children said they were sexually abused in U.S. detention centers, report says.* Retrieved from https://www.nytimes.com/2019/02/27/us/immigrant-children-sexual-abuse.html.

Makarechi, K. (2018, June 21). *These kids are traumatized: For migrant children caught at the border, detention is just the beginning.* Retrieved from https://www.vanityfair.com/news/2018/06/what-happens-to-immigrant-kids-once-theyre-released?verso=true.

Simha, S. (2019, March 1). *The Impact of family separation on immigrant and refugee families.* Retrieved from http://www.ncmedicaljournal.com/content/80/2/95.full.

Wikipedia. (2019, June 19). *"Cadejo".* Retrieved from https://en.wikipedia.org/wiki/Cadejo.

Chapter 17: The Secret

Fernandez, M. (2019, March 3). *You have to pay with your body: The Hidden nightmare of sexual violence on the border.* Retrieved from https://www.nytimes.com/2019/03/03/us/border-rapes-migrant-women.html.

Goldberg, E. (2017, December 6). *80% of Central American women, girls are raped crossing Into the U.S.* Retrieved from https://www.huff-post.com/entry/central-america-migrants-rape_n_5806972.

mzbitca. (2009, March 26). *Rape trees and immigrant women: The Silent victims.* Retrieved from https://mzbitca.wordpress.com/2009/03/26/rape-trees-and-immigrant-women-the-silent-victims/.

Chapter 18: Welcome to the U.S.

Customs and Immigration Services. (2019, June 20). *Annual report: Immigration enforcement actions, 2017.* Retrieved from https://cis.org/sites/default/files/2019-05/Immigration%20Enforcement%20Actions%202017.pdf.

International Rescue Committee. (2019, March 1). *Is it legal to cross the U.S. border to seek asylum?* Retrieved from https://www.rescue.org/article/it-legal-cross-us-border-seek-asylum.

Justice for Immigrants. (2019, June 20). *Family detention.* Retrieved from https://justiceforimmigrants.org/what-we-are-working-on/immigrant-detention/family-detention/.

Karas, T. (2018, May 1). *How does seeking asylum work at the US border?* Retrieved from https://www.pri.org/stories/2018-05-01/how-does-seeking-asylum-work-us-border.

Regnaud, D. (2018, June 27). *Inside a Texas "stash house" where smugglers house dozens of immigrants.* Retrieved from https://www.cbsnews.com/news/inside-a-texas-stash-house-where-smugglers-house-dozens-of-immigrants/.

U.S. Citizenship and Immigration Services. (2019, June 20). *Credible fear FAQs.* Retrieved from https://www.uscis.gov/faq-page/credible-fear-faq#t12831n40211.

Chapter 19. Detention

American Immigration Council. (2018, May 14). *Asylum in the United States.* Retrieved from https://www.americanimmigrationcouncil.org/research/asylum-united-states.

American Immigration Council, (2018, September). *Legal orientation program overview.* Retrieved from https://www.americanimmigrationcouncil.org/research/legal-orientation-program-overview.

Associated Press. (2018, December 8). *Honduran woman in migrant caravan gives birth in US.* Retrieved from https://www.apnews.com/3ca21d8faf414f639693f07fbf4bc7ea.

Benevento, M. ((2018, December 21). *Legal representation for detained migrants hindered by access issues.* Retrieved from https://www.ncronline.org/news/justice/legal-representation-detained-migrants-hindered-access-issues.

Bixby, S. (2018, August 20). *Detained dads: ICE re-separated our families as punishment.* Retrieved from https://www.thedailybeast.com/detained-dads-ice-re-separated-our-families-as-punishment.

Contreras, G. (2018, August 18). *Inside the country's largest immigrant family detention center.* Retrieved from https://www.expressnews.com/news/local/article/Inside-the-country-s-largest-immigrant-family-13149672.php.

Gamboa, S. (2019, May 8). *Trump administration is blocking immigrants from free legal help, attorneys allege.* Retrieved from https://www.nbcnews.com/news/latino/trump-administration-blocking-immigrants-free-legal-help-attorneys-allege-n1003516.

Garbus, M. (2019, March 26). *What I saw at the Dilley, Texas, immigrant detention center.* Retrieved from https://www.thenation.com/article/dilley-texas-immigration-detention/.

Kaufmann, G. ((2017, October 12). *Pregnant immigrants say they've been denied medical care in detention centers.* Retrieved from https://www.thenation.com/article/pregnant-immigrants-say-theyve-been-denied-medical-care-in-detention-centers/.

National Immigrant Justice Center. (2019, June 20). *Access to counsel.* Retrieved from https://www.immigrantjustice.org/issues/access-counsel.

National Immigrant Justice Center. (2019, June 20). *Asylum project intake questions.* Retrieved from http://immigrantjustice.org/sites/immigrantjustice.org/files/BestPracticesManual_2.%20NIJC%20Asylum%20Project%20Intake%20Questions.pdf.

Powers, C. (2018, August 23). *I spent 5 days at a family detention center. I'm still haunted by what I saw.* Retrieved from https://www.huffpost.com/entry/family-detention-center-border_n_5b7c2673e4b0a5b1febf3abf.

United States Citizenship and Immigration Services. (2019, June 20). *Credible fear workload report summary FY 2017 total caseload.* Retrieved from https://www.uscis.gov/sites/default/files/USCIS/Outreach/Upcoming%20National%20Engagements/PED_FY17_CFandRFstatsThru09302017.pdf.

Woodruff, B. (2018, August 18). *ICE is detaining a woman who is 32 weeks pregnant.* Retrieved from https://www.thedailybeast.com/ice-is-detaining-a-woman-who-is-32-weeks-pregnant.

Yahr, N. (2019, May 20). *Stuck in detention: For immigrants without lawyers, justice is hard to find.* Retrieved from https://www.mprnews.org/story/2019/05/20/stuck-in-detention-for-immigrants-without-lawyers-justice-is-hard-to-find.

Zazueta-Castro, L. (2019, May 2). *Donna tent facility reopens to accommodate asylum-seekers; lawmakers seek to add port officers.* Retrieved from https://www.themonitor.com/2019/05/02/donna-tent-facility-reopens-accommodate-asylum-seekers-lawmakers-seek-add-port-officers/.

Chapter 20: What's Next?

AllLaw. (2019, June 20). *Appeals process after a denied asylum application.* Retrieved from https://www.alllaw.com/articles/nolo/us-immigration/appeals-process-denied-asylum-application.html.

Arland-Fye, B. ((2019, May 9). *On anniversary of immigration raid, Iowans join in solidarity, prayer.* Retrieved from https://www. ncronline.org/news/justice/anniversary-immigration-raid-iowans-join-solidarity-prayer.

Howland, L. (2019, May 31). *Vacant Turlock church to house migrant families seeking asylum.* Retrieved from https://www.abc10.com/article/news/local/turlock/vacant-turlock-church-to-house-migrant-families-seeking-asylum/103-c153f5b2-2148-4538-a079-6948e42e39c5.

TRACReports, Inc. (2019, June 20). *Average time pending cases have been waiting in immigration courts as of May 2019.* Retrieved from https://trac.syr.edu/phptools/immigration/court_backlog/apprep_backlog_avgdays.php.

Epilogue: Fields of Dreams

French, A. (2018, February 2). *'In the Fields of the North' reveals the reality of migrant farm workers.* Retrieved from https://www.latimes. com/books/la-ca-jc-fields-of-the-north-20180202-story.html.

Skelton, G. (2019, May 20). *Thanks to immigrants, California is changing for the better before our eyes.* Retrieved from https://www. latimes.com/politics/la-pol-sac-skelton-immigration-ppic-california-20190520-story.html.

A CALL TO ACTION

Shortly before *Desperate Trek* went to press, the news media exploded with the revelation that Central American children being held in U.S. detention centers weren't provided with the basic necessities of life and daily hygiene: adequate water, food, beds, medical care, toothbrushes, soap or diapers. The news was heartbreaking for many Americans and reinforced my commitment to the growing chorus of those demanding change in our immigration system.

When the photo surfaced of the father and young daughter who drowned trying to cross the Rio Grande River, my editor and I decided to add this Call to Action to the book. We need to reckon with all that stands in the way of world citizens of any age arriving to the U.S. safely. To insist that "they should come to the U.S. the right way" discounts the desperation each migrant carries with them on their trek. Complying with proper procedures is understandably not the primary concern for those escaping extortion, rape, violence, and the threat of murder.

This book cannot keep pace with fast-changing current events in the immigration crisis on the southern border. We continue to be alarmed and angered at the daily revelations about conditions at our detention centers and how broken our immigration system is. We imagine that you feel as we do. What can we do from so far away?

One way of helping is to make monetary donations to charities that are trying to assist immigrants with shelter, safety, and support. Some of these organizations are listed below. Please note that I am not making any claim about these organizations. You should conduct research with due diligence before giving to any charity.

- **RAICES** - promotes justice by providing free and low-cost legal services to underserved immigrant children, families, and refugees.
https://www.raicestexas.org

- **Al Otro Lado** - serves indigent deportees, migrants, and refugees in Tijuana & Los Angeles.
https://www.alotrolado.org

- **The Florence Project** - providing legal & social services to detained immigrants in Arizona.
https://firrp.org/

- **Innovation Law Lab** - working in immigrant detention centers and hostile judicial districts; keeping the definitive list of immigrant children being held.
https://www.innovationlawlab.org

- **The Young Center for Immigrant Children's Rights** - promoting the best interests of unaccompanied immigrant children.
https://www.theyoungcenter.org/

- **Families Belong Together** - fighting for common sense immigration policies & reuniting families.
http://www.webelongtogether.org/

- **United We Dream** - the largest immigrant youth-led network in the country.
https://unitedwedream.org/

- **Women's Refugee Commission** - advocating for the rights and protection of women, children, and youth fleeing violence and persecution. https://www.womensrefugeecommission.org/

- **ACLU** - fighting attacks through the legal system. http://www.aclu.org

- **Kids In Need of Defense (KIND)** - protecting unaccompanied children who enter the US immigration system alone to ensure that no child appears in court without an attorney. https://supportkind.org/

- **Asylum Seeker Advocacy Project** - providing asylum seekers with legal aid and community support across the country. https://asylumadvocacy.org/

- **Human Rights First** - helping refugees obtain asylum in the U.S. https://www.humanrightsfirst.org/

- **La Union del Pueblo Entero** - founded by Cesar Chavez and Dolores Huerta, a community union that works in the Rio Grande Valley from the grassroots up. https://lupenet.org/

- **Save the Children** - working to deliver immediate humanitarian aid to migrant children and families. The organization is working with local partners to ensure that children and families have necessities such as hygiene kits, diapers and clothing.
https://www.savethechildren.org

- **Catholic Charities** - advocates for immigration and refugee policies that protect family unity and allow newcomers an opportunity to contribute and participate more fully in our communities.
https://www.catholiccharitiesusa.org